Praise for the
Taxi For the Dead Mysteries

"If you like your mystery with a paranormal edge, then you should be reading this series." ~Cheryl Green

Praise for Renaissance Faire Mysteries

"**Fatal Fairies** was a good read. I loved being back at the Renaissance Faire Village with Jessie, Chase and all of the village characters. I like the magical twist that happens to Jessie in this book and I'm curious to see what other magic happens in future books. Thank you Joyce and Jim for writing a great story that transported me to a village I wouldn't mind living in! Eagerly awaiting the next book in the series!" ~ **R. Davila**

Praise for Missing Pieces Mysteries

"I really enjoyed **A Watery Death**, it was full of a few surprises and a very nice guest appearance that was fun to read about. As well as a nice surprise but sad guest appearance to enjoy. Can't wait for the next book!" ~ **April Schilling**

Praise for the Retired Witches Mysteries

"**Spell Booked** kept me guessing. Who was good, who could be trusted, and who was the rogue witch? Joyce and James Lavene created a world where magic and mundane live together yet separate-even in the same households." ~ **Cozy Up With Kathy**

Gone By Midnight
and other stories
By
Joyce and Jim Lavene

Lavene,
Joyce

Copyright © 2016 Joyce and Jim Lavene

Book coach and editor — Jeni Chappelle
http://www.jenichappelle.com/

Acknowledgments:
The authors want to acknowledge Jeni Chappelle for her editorial skills to help get this book to print and Emily Andreis and Chris Lavene for their support and proof reading skills.

Dedication:
In loving memory of Joyce Lavene who passed away on October 20, 2015

We will miss her and hope her memory and works live on as she would want them to.

Preface

My parents started writing together in the 1980s. But before that, they drove the back roads in northern Minnesota and later rural North Carolina, telling each other stories, making them more and more elaborate. This became their primary way of plotting for years and was their go-to for tricky story issues, even after they'd published dozens of novels.

But learning to write books as a team took some time. Before they wrote their first novel together, they wrote dozens of stories and articles of all genres to practice and hone their process. They'd discuss the plots, characters, settings, and ideas they wanted to express in the stories, all before they'd start the new story. It was always fun to see them become animated with a cry of "Oh! What if we did this…" or "I have a crazy idea."

Gone by Midnight is a compilation of some of those stories, plus others written in the worlds of their bestselling series. Some of these stories may make you smile, and some may make you cry. A few may even scare you!

But in them, you'll see so much of what readers have come to love about my parents' writing: complex characters, families with heart, descriptions that evoke not only the facts of a place but also the way it feels. Many are set in the American South, where my parents have lived most of their lives. But maybe not the way we all know it. My parents see the mystery and magic of a place and bring it to life on the page.

Lucky us, that we get to share in it.

Jeni Chappelle, Editor
March 2016

Aunt Edna

Set in the same world as the Missing Pieces series, this story reminds us to learn from the ghosts of the past without fear. Bankers—as folks from the Outer Banks call themselves—have worked hard for centuries to live amidst the shifting sands and changing inlets. They have weathered storm surges, hurricanes, and shipwrecks. And some few still linger to tell their tales.

There wasn't ever a time Aunt Edna didn't have a piece of pie for you to eat while you were at her home, usually on the front porch swing, and a pie to take with you. She was an obsessive baker. Even after Uncle Charlie died, she still made those pies that had won blue ribbons for forty years. You could smell the aroma of them drifting down the beach. They were a constant, like the shush-shush of the tide and the breathtaking sunset.

Her kinfolk came and took her to a home for her own good when she was close to one hundred. They figured her gnarled old hands had turned enough crust and sliced enough apples. She argued and lamented, but in the end, it became a fact.

The old clapboard house that had needed a coat of paint for twenty years stood empty until her death. The sand crept in where she had once shooed it with her broom, and the seagulls built nests in the chimney that led from the old stove. A hurricane came through and ripped away the porch, leaving the swing dangling by its chain above the sand.

After Edna's death, her children sold the property to a development corporation. Edna wouldn't sign over the house, stubborn to the end, and just a touch bitter over being taken from her home. Like the tide takes the sand each day, it was only a matter of time for her loved ones. Eventually, they were able to buy their boats and cruises and diamonds while their children waited for their turn.

They built a fine apartment building where her house had been, and people forgot that the pie lady had ever lived there. Old people died, and new people came to live along that stretch of the gray Atlantic. The apartments were leased, and if, from time to time, there was the aroma of baking pies wafting through the hallways, no one thought much about it.

It wasn't until Mrs. Dalton from 2B saw a woman standing at her stove that people started saying the place was haunted. Mrs. Dalton screamed, and the woman at the stove smiled at her and turned to mist. Mrs. Dalton dropped to the floor like a stone.

A young woman came to live in 2B after Mrs. Dalton hastily sought a new place to live. Her name was Elise Walters. She was a quiet, private person, who'd decided as a child to look down at the ground rather than risk meeting people's eyes as she passed them. She liked to read and cook, although most of the time she was alone and it hardly seemed worth the effort.

She kept to herself, and no one was sure about her name or what she did for a living. They talked about her, as people will when they don't know the facts, making things up that suited them.

One night after midnight, Elise was awakened by the distinct sound of humming and the strong smell of apple pie. The cinnamon made her mouth water.

She put on her glasses and crept from her room into the dark apartment, wondering which of her neighbors were baking at that hour. Because she didn't know their names, she called them Mr. Angel Hair for the corona of white hair on his head and his beatific expression and Mrs. Good Body because she was always in workout clothes. It didn't seem to Elise that neither one of them was a likely suspect in the pie-baking.

Her mouth was dry. She yawned and went to the kitchen for a glass of water. Half awake, she filled a glass and put it to her lips, raising her eyes to the kitchen around her. The glass slipped from her hand and fell to the floor, shattering with a cascade of water.

Standing at her stove was a figure of a woman. She was busily doing something with her hands. Elise could plainly see that her back was turned to her, yet the woman had no more substance than a mist from the ocean. She had no feet and appeared to be floating on a cushion of air. The humming sound was coming from her. Her little white-haired head bobbed up and down, while her hands moved back and forth.

"W-who are you?" Elise asked.

The woman didn't turn around right away. She kept working on whatever the unseen project was before her. She stopped humming, and that made Elise bolder.

"Who are you?"

The woman turned then, and her smile was as sweet as the scent of apple pie that surrounded her. She tilted her head and looked right back at Elise. She didn't speak, but Elise had the feeling that it was all right. She wasn't sure what was all right, but she felt secure and warm in a way she'd never felt before.

Her stomach grumbled, and the woman smiled at her again. She was hungry too.

Every night for a week, Elise got up to watch the old lady working. She came to understand that she was making the pies whose scent permeated the building. They weren't real, of course, but several times she'd heard her neighbors comment on the wonderful aroma. Mrs. Good Body didn't like it because it made her hungry. Mr. Angel Hair loved it because he was happy to feed that hunger, even at midnight.

Elise had never made a pie in her life, but her fingers itched to try. She bought flour, a pie pan, and canned apple filling. She sat down at the table with a cookbook, but it was as though she didn't need it. She knew everything she needed to do. The old lady shook her head when Elise poured in the apple filling.

"Next time, I'll buy the apples," she promised. "I wasn't even sure I could make the crust!"

The pie was baking, and the aroma was even more tantalizing than the ghostly scent. Elise strolled out on her balcony, which looked out at the wide expanse of shoreline from pier to pier in the hazy distance. Children laughed as they played, and their parents strolled the water's edge. Seabirds called out as they wheeled through the late summer sky. Elise looked at her balcony and found herself wondering if there was any way she could put up a swing.

A knock sounded on her door. She checked her pie, but it was just starting to turn a golden shade of brown. Juice bubbled up thick and sweet. The knock repeated itself, and she went to answer it. It was a tall, broad-shouldered man with dark brown hair and eyes the color of the morning sky. For a minute they just looked at each other.

Then he collected himself and smiled. It was as good and as sweet as the juice bubbling up from Elise's pie.

"Hi. We don't know each other, but I live in 2C."

That was Mrs. Good Body's apartment. Elise considered that she just couldn't take the temptation the ghost lady's pies presented any more.

"Yes?"

"I was wondering... I know this sounds lame, but could I borrow a cup of sugar? I could smell your pies baking, so I thought you'd be a good bet until I could get to the store tomorrow. I just moved in, and I can't seem to find anything."

Elise smiled, and for once, she didn't look down. Her pretty, brown eyes crinkled up at the corners, like it was something she did every day. "Of course. I have a slice of pie and some milk, if you'd like some."

He nodded, feeling right at home with her, like he'd always been there, like they'd always been together. "I'd like that."

"Good. Come in and sit down. It should be ready in a few minutes. You can take the rest of it home with you."

"No, I couldn't take it all! You just baked it."

"I'll be baking again tomorrow," she said softly. "Maybe blueberry next time."

They sat across from each other, and the pie lady smiled. From the open doorway came the shush-shush of the water lapping on the sand, and the breathtaking sunset burst upon the sky.

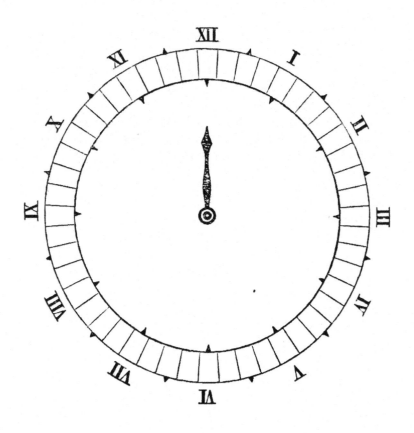

Inn of Many Pleasures

As huge fantasy fans, we know of few things better than a tale of high intrigue and triumph over evil. An itinerant storyteller, a roaring fire, old wine in pewter mugs, and skewers of roasted meat; we can almost imagine the Table of the Five Merchants in some back corner of the Lady in the Lake Tavern on the shore of the pirate lagoon in The Renaissance Faire Village & Marketplace. Enjoy yourself, but watch out for pickpockets, thieves, and a rose-hilted sword...

"I tell you she's nothing but a myth," Ba'kar the merchant said zealously, clapping his heavy silver mug on the table.

There was laughter from around the table where the Five Merchants sat, ruminating over their drinks and old men's tales. The youngest, Plinor, sat stroking his thin beard, which he valued only slightly less than his life.

"It seems to me that there are many stories about her for her to be fiction," he conjectured wisely.

Mellan, the eldest, nodded sagely. "For once I agree with the boy."

Plinor winced at the title.

"Bah! Tales to scare old men with feeble minds." Ba'kar glanced at the senior merchant.

Mellan refused to look at the other man who so coveted

his position with the queen. "I have seen her myself. Seriana, our most Reverent Majesty, has spoken to me on occasion."

It was a lie but, hopefully, one big enough only to satisfy his companions with his importance to the queen but not enough to bring his ruler's notice.

"Where did you see her?" Raj insisted, leaning slightly forward toward the older man.

"In the palace once on a stormy winter night." Mellan's eyes grew misty and far away. He recalled the vision he had beheld with a slight trembling in his voice. "She brushed by me in the corridor. I felt death around me."

"They say she is beautiful." Raj, the romantic, sighed into his spiced wine.

"They say so much about her." Brun tended to agree with Ba'kar. "How can anyone credit any of it?"

"I didn't see her face," Mellan continued as though he had never stopped. "The red-hooded cloak kept her face and form in shadow."

"Then how, pray, Mellan, did you know that it was the infamous Eris herself?" Ba'kar demanded with an assured glance at Brun.

"The light from the taper in the wall shone out on the hilt of her sword that held the cape back from her right side. It was the ruby rose insignia, inscribed in gold."

There was a hush over the group as they considered the deeds that had been attributed to the sword.

Ba'kar had heard enough. "I still say, stuff of dreams and bad food! Let me hear a story that truly sounds as if a real person could have done it and not some witch whore with a rose-hilted sword!"

"More wine!" Brun slapped the table.

A serving wench appeared with a large pouring vessel of the strong, amber wine. Raj held his nose as she neared, the stench of her nearly gagging him. Ba'kar roared for some livelier sport than the old crone and gave her a sharp kick to the ribs. She rolled to the floor, grasping her side and coughing, her rags spread around her with the rest of the pitcher of wine.

The innkeeper hurried the old wretch on her way back to the kitchen and smiled pleasantly at the Five Merchants. After every journey they made for the queen, they stopped at the Inn of Many Pleasures. They were loud and frequently destructive, but there were few who were not at the inn—and as well for they had no money.

The innkeeper queried politely if all was to their satisfaction. His reply was a shout for more meat.

"My uncle, who is now retired from the service, said that he met Eris face to face." Plinor smiled. "Or rather, sword to throat. She took a single pearl from him that earned him fifty lashes."

"Why is it that she steals only jewels?" Brun knew that if he were a thief, he would steal anything of value.

Ba'kar growled at him for getting caught up in the fantasy.

"Because of her beauty," Raj replied dreamily. "She is like a jewel herself."

"They say that she is the queen's sister, her older sister, turned outlaw. That is why, when their parents were so cruelly murdered, Seriana undertook the responsibilities of the throne in her early youth." Mellan explained what he had heard muttered by a drunken steward as though it were the teachings of the law.

The old woman came again with meat and more wine, balanced precariously in her hands. Ba'kar yelled that the meat tasted like the old woman smelled and shoved her roughly away again, calling for another server.

"She is the only one I have tonight." The innkeeper tried to placate him. "But I will bring the meat myself."

The inn was noisy around the group gathered at the table. From time to time, as is practice at such establishments, a fight would break out. Tables would roll, angry words would be slurred from less than steady mouths.

In the kitchen, where the smell of roasted lamb was ever-present, a new load of wine was being delivered. There was shouting and swearing as a keg broke open and the kitchen help fell to the floor to lap it up like dogs. Outside, the sun was setting, shadowing the city with rosy hues that softened the mountain landscape and fired the sky with brilliance. Children begged in the streets, and the queen's guard rode by on their dashing mounts. The stench of the old and the infirm mingled with the perfume of many flowers and the odor of the new things that Seriana had brought to her parents' city.

"In the meantime…" A young man gracefully strolled to their table. "A story, perhaps?"

"We've heard enough of stories," Ba'kar grumbled, drinking deeply of his cup. "Let's hear a little of the truth."

"Well, if it's the truth about Eris," the storyteller smiled knowledgeably. "I am the one to ask."

"You know of Eris?" Plinor asked in awe.

"Know of her?" The young man in green velvet laughed. "I tell you that I met Eris. Here in this very place, less than a year ago. She herself told me the tale I am about to tell you." He leveled a glance at Ba'kar's scowling face. "And I promise you that it will sound as though a real person had done it."

"Tell us," Raj begged, tossing a handful of gold to the other man. "What does she look like?"

The storyteller pocketed his gold and caught each man's eye that he might make his tale more convincing. When even rude Ba'kar was looking at him, a plate of fresh meat set before him, he began to tell his story. The inn seemed to become hushed, and the men sipped slowly of their wine.

"It was not so long ago, in a land that bordered a great white sea, a prince lived, who, because of various misfortunes, had made a pact with a lesser devil. In exchange for his land's prosperity, a great beast haunted his court, gorging itself on human flesh," he began.

The prince was a tall, commanding man, savage in battle and fair in his judgements on his people. They say that he was as glorious to look at as any man has ever been, with hair the color of sunlight and eyes as dark as night. He never married, never allowed himself to lay with a woman because he believed that the practice was detrimental. Needless to say, he was a man of considerable will and strength. His princedom grew and prospered.

Now the people of this land loved their prince, even though his promise to the devil seemed quite strange to them. Still, he was a wise man, and while his beast's grisly habits might have turned the people against him in time had it eaten, say, an entire family, the prince primed its palate for strangers who were unlucky enough to be caught traveling through his land. The people could ignore such a thing. After all, what was a stranger to them but possibly trouble?

Who is to say what drew Eris to this land? There were rumors of a fabulous cache of jewels that the lesser devil had given the prince. Or it could have been that she was simply passing through that place on the way to another.

Whatever it was, they found her seated at a road post, some distance into the princedom. She wore a red cloak, easily recognized in the gray and brown countryside. It must be assumed that she feared nothing, for her raiment gave her no camouflage such as most seek when they travel.

The prince's guards, at least ten of them, came upon her while on patrol.

"You are a stranger," the captain spoke savagely.

"This place must be quite small," she observed at once, a ghost of a smile on her lips, "for you to know everyone who is or is not a stranger."

The captain looked meaningfully at Eris's red cloak. "I believe I should remember one such as you."

"Perhaps I am a visiting relative or newlywed wife," Eris retorted. "Would you know me then, captain?"

The man was clearly put out. "Are you a stranger then?"

Eris laughed, the sound like chimes in the wind. "Am I? I know myself quite well. You, on the other hand, seem quite strange to me, captain."

"You play games. Strangers are not allowed in this land. Either you will identify yourself or you must be taken to the prince." The captain glanced at the long sword, shielded at her side, and the knife in her boot.

"Prince Radir," she said. "The fair and the wise. In his palace beside the white sea."

"You know of him?" The man was almost relieved. "You must be one of us."

"No," Eris smiled, shaking her head. "I'm afraid I've never been here before. But it seems a delightful place."

The captain balked, confused and surprised, yet before he could give the order that she be taken, Eris moved like a brisk breeze, her knife at his throat.

"I shall go with you to the palace, but only on my own terms. Captain, your men must lose their horses and drop their swords, or your life is forfeit."

The captain, clearly believing what the woman, surely a witch woman, told him, knew that he feared her more than the prince. The prince could only kill him once; a witch could curse him for eternity.

He gave the order, and while his men were slow to follow, eventually, they all did so. One or two might have eyed the captain's position with his own favor to be gained if he disobeyed and attacked, but the prince's edict read death for anyone who did not obey for any reason. Better to follow and live, they agreed grudgingly. After all, how much of one's life could be risked at the rate of pay they received each month?

The captain mounted, astonished when Eris was immediately behind him on the horse. The prick of her knife in his back was not surprising, though, and he urged the beast toward the palace at top speed. The red cloak flew out behind Eris on the white horse, the last thing the men saw of them before they disappeared over the hills.

Did the soldiers find their horses or walk back? Perhaps you wonder. But that is not part of my story.

Eris, however, reached the palace with the captain for escort. She kept the man before her as the gates were lifted and the palace opened to them like a dewy flower. They dismounted as one and crossed the empty courtyard on silent feet in the gathering dusk.

Prince Radir and his courtiers were in the throne room of gold floors, ivory walls, and the great, jade throne. The prince was resplendent in jewels and satin, lace-edged collar at his throat. His beauty was magnificent, and he had gathered around him a retinue of equally beautiful creatures. Nothing crippled or ugly was left in his sight for long.

So it was when the triple doors burst open and his captain released that he gasped when he beheld the beauty who had gained entrance to his throne room in such an unseemly manner.

Eris threw her cloak back from her shoulders regally. Her black boots were highly polished despite the road dust, her slender legs encased in white fawn-skin breeches. Her shirt was black and of the purest silk but not a rival to the pearlescent sheen of her skin as she bowed low and the neck of her shirt parted slightly to reveal the upper curves of her breasts. Her neck was long and slender, as were her hands. Her black hair was unbound as the night and full of starry lights as it dropped down her back and shoulders. Her eyes were bright sapphires, and her mouth a bow of rubies. Even in that room of splendid, lovely faces and forms, she shone like a new moon.

"Who are you?" Prince Radir asked in both awe and speculation.

"Your Highness," she smiled. "I am Eris."

The crowd of courtiers drew slightly more hushed. They had heard this name. A few saw the gold filigree around the ruby rose on her sword.

"Not of this land." The prince nodded. "We have a heavy toll for strangers to pay. What brings you here?"

"The black diamond at your highness's throat," she replied simply. "I am a collector of rare and valuable jewels."

"You wish to buy it." The prince laughed outright.

"Of course not," she answered coolly. "I wish to steal it."

There was no sound. Even the fountains grew silent.

"Strangers here are never welcome yet always needed, as there is a curse on this land," the prince told her. "When you ventured here, Eris, you met your last adventure."

"Only one thing I request, your highness," Eris replied craftily, cool and sweet as spring breezes. "Your beast. Can you loose it to meet me, here in the throne room?"

The prince stared, his mind turning. What did it matter? Let everyone behold that even this sword bearer could have no power over the beast. Let them know—and fear.

"Very well," he agreed. "It matters little to me. And we would enjoy the sport."

An audible gasp escaped the crowd, followed by a buzz of voices. Few had ever seen the beast. Fewer still had seen it kill.

The prince pushed a large, gilt button on the wall. The sound of something heavy sliding, stone across stone, brought the courtiers into a frightened huddle at the far end of the throne room as the golden floor parted. A deep crevasse yawned into blackness that was fetid and frightening.

Eris stood calmly, almost negligibly. One could expect her to yawn of boredom at any moment. She did not even touch her rose-hilted sword. Yet there was a wariness in her eyes.

One moment the beast was not there; the next he was in the center of the room, green, gray, and red with scaled body and claw-like hands. His eyes searched for his victim. His mouth drooled when he found her, easily marked in blood red. He began to slither toward her, tail slapping from side to side.

A few fainted. Some were sick. Most watched in hypnotic terror. The prince leaned forward on his throne, the black diamond Eris was so fond of hanging from his throat.

Eris eased her blade from its sheath as the creature approached, throwing her small knife swiftly and surely to the thing's left side. It bellowed, but there was no blood. The knife was plucked out and tossed away like a toy.

Blue eyes flashed intuitively, Eris made a few passes at the lumbering creature with her sword. Then swiftly, almost thoughtlessly, she leaped, not at the creature but at the prince. Before anyone could move or blink astonished eyes, she'd separated his head from his body with her sword.

There was no blood. The head rolled to one side, and the body fell forward to the ivory stairs that led to the throne. The creature collapsed on top of him, soundlessly. Then was no more than mist.

Eris slowly wiped her blade on the prince's elegant raiment.

"How did you know?" The captain of the guard demanded, not certain what to do but certain of what he had seen.

"Your prince obviously lost himself to the demon long ago. It simply ruled in his place." She sheathed her blade and took the black diamond from the fallen body with a   delicate hand. "For a meat-eating creature, the thing had remarkably flat teeth, while the prince's teeth were sharply pointed and unusually long. It was he who ate your strangers. And, too, it came for me. Not for any of you. It knew that I was the target because someone was directing it. The illusion was merely a facade for the real demon." She smiled, like watersilk rushing away. "And now you are free."

"Free," a man repeated, looking at the prince's body.

"He was a good man," a woman mourned, shaking her head.

"A lover of beauty," said another.

Eris shook her head over the whims of man and womankind and chained the black crystal around her throat. She pulled her cloak around her, and when next they thought to look, she was gone.

"The stone came to rest in that most enviable spot between the full white mounds of her breasts. It was there that I beheld it, and I can tell you that it was not an ordinary stone." The storyteller took a draft of wine.

"Of course not." Ba'kar spoke at last, shaking himself from the thralls of the story. "A black diamond—any black diamond—is a rare and costly stone."

"So she is as beautiful as I have heard," Raj breathed.

"A very good story." Mellan cleared his throat and looked at the storyteller's handsome face. "I have heard that Eris was nearly killed for her evil by our own queen."

The storyteller laughed, showing perfect white teeth. "Ah! But that is another story, friend!"

Brun still could not believe. "If that is so and Eris cannot resist jewels, then how is it that our treasure has slipped by her since it would be of particular notice to her?"

"Brun! Your tongue runs away with you," Mellan cautioned.

"We carry jewels that will make up Queen Seriana's crown for her coronation," Plinor confided eagerly.

"It is common knowledge." Ba'kar belched, calling for more wine. When it arrived, he was quick to backhand the serving wench for spilling a drop on his suit. "So much for your myth of Eris the bandit."

There was a scuffle close to the Merchants' table that overturned chairs and mugs, sending tables rolling across the floor. The old woman shrieked and fell into the center, right where their table had been before the commotion. The innkeeper begged for peace, while most of the other occupants of the inn watched in drunken curiosity.

Ba'kar forcefully threw the old woman down the stairs

toward the kitchen, where the innkeeper completed her fall.

"Get in there and don't show your face again here," he yelled, feeling that the whole scene could have been avoided if she had not been so clumsy.

Plinor and Raj set the table up again on its stand. In a crack in the wood at its center, there was a newly budded red rose.

"What nonsense is this?" Brun demanded, looking for his cup. "A rose?"

The Five Merchants looked across at one another. They each felt at his side for the heavy leather purse that held Seriana's jewels, gathered from her far flung empire.

"My soul," Mellan swore softly as he found it gone.

"She exists!" Brun hardly dared to speak. "And she has stolen the queen's jewels."

"And our lives, half brain," Ba'kar declared, lumbering to his feet. "The old woman! Yes, it was the old woman!"

"I have heard that she uses disguises often," Plinor agreed.

"After her," Mellan shouted, the only one of the Five to truly understand what their failure would mean.

How much more could the queen's jewels be worth than a mere pearl that Eris had stolen from Plinor's uncle? They would not live to see the day out, yet when death came, they would be grateful.

He ran out after the others, who had located a division of Seriana's guard and already scoured the area for the old woman.

The storyteller shook his head and smiled only slightly. He left the inn and blended with the crowd on the blackened city streets. In time, he would don a red cloak and the red rose would gleam in ruby and gold on his sword. On her sword.

Eris felt the jewels weigh down her velvet pockets and the beautiful storyteller was no more. Her sapphire eyes looked towards the east as she left the city.

And, alas, they would not find the old woman in the twisted morass of the city streets that night or any other. She had played her part and been given a purse of gold and a swift horse, leaving the city behind her. Her grandchildren would laugh over her story.

Ghost Dance

Visions have inspired the many prophets and medicine men to greater healing and prosperity for their communities. What are the origins of these visions? How should they be interpreted? This story about the Ghost Dance is set in the world of the Christmas Tree Valley mysteries. It takes place between the Trail of Tears and when the tribes began to make their way back east of the Mississippi. It is our explanation of these visions, but it may not be true. But, then, who can know the ways of the Great Spirit?

The men are dancing. The flames soar high into the black sky. The gray smoke rises to heaven and feeds the wrath of God.

It is good.

"Where is he?" they whisper in the shadows. Their eyes cast anxiously across the distance. The women sit, keeping the babies quiet. The fire spits and sizzles.

A man is coming—Wovoka, the prophet, the powerful medicine man from the southeast plains. The Great Spirit has spoken to him. He will make a new world. He will roll up the old world. The iron snake will be destroyed, and the whispering wire will be stilled.

The white man will be gone.

He raises his hands. The singing is quiet. Even the wind pauses to listen.

"In two years, there will be a happy world," the prophet says, "with green fields. Food for all. The buffalo will return. And the Dead Ones will be here with us—mothers, sisters, sons, brothers."

The flames roar. The dancers cry out until the night echoes with their shouting. The women cry silently, burying their faces in the sleeping warmth of their children.

The prophet nods and watches, Wovoka in his thin shirt, his gaunt frame illuminated by the fire. His hair is gray and thin as the old wolf, blown by the wind. He wears a single white feather. The Great Spirit will know by this that he is one of the People. He will not be destroyed when the world is made new.

"The night is cold," his wife says. "What will become of us?"

The white man does not like the Ghost Dance. Wovoka knows that they feared the singing, the wild dancing in the night.

The chiefs meet in secrecy, uncertain what the future holds. They beg Wovoka to see the end of it all.

He cannot answer.

The white man could go of his own accord, back across the big water, or he could be destroyed. It mattered little.

"I have known many good white men," Wovoka acknowledged. He would like to see them escape.

The others had brought stink and disease. They had lied and killed.

"Let them die," the chiefs spoke, their lips pulled tight.

The Great Spirit spoke to Wovoka almost two years ago, in the fall of 1888. It was just before the shadow passed over the sun. They must dance each month for four days. They would always wear a feather.

In return, by the end of 1890, the white man would be gone. The new world, with its promise of peace and plenty, would be shown to them.

Wovoka alone saw the new world. He brought the word

to his brothers.

"Tell us," they demanded. "Tell us how this happened to you."

He awakened, startled. A Christian farmer had read him the Bible years before, and he'd found himself dreaming about demons. They were demons he knew—famine, thirst, war, fear. They all gnawed at him as they did at his brothers.

Closer every day they were pushed to the brink of extinction. Even the mighty warriors, the Sioux and the Cheyenne, hid in the shadows, fearful and full of sorrow.

Wovoka got out of his bed, looking out his tiny window at the pasture below. The land slept around him.

The pain started in his head again. He got down on his knees and prayed to God and the Great Spirit, their son-brother Jesus, to relieve him of this agony. A white hot arrow of pain thrust through his head. Sweat beaded his lip as he fought to control his torture as a man. His body bent double to the rough wooden floor. Wovoka fought for breath.

Then suddenly, it was gone. Warily, he raised his head, fearing its return.

But where was he? There was a round, yellow light in the ceiling, and the room was warm around him. The floor had been roughhewn boards where he had crouched low but now there was a flat fur upon it. It was strange to the touch of his hand. In one corner, there were large, white boxes, one tall, one squat. And before him was a man with flowing, white hair and weathered face, a large eagle-headed walking stick in his gnarled hand.

It could only be the Great Spirit. Wovoka came to his feet at once. He would be seen as a man.

The old man peered at him with eyes as old as ages. "Who are you?"

Wovoka raised his head. "I am Wovoka."

"Why have you come?"

He thought. "To tell my brothers that you have not forsaken us. To give them hope."

The old man nodded.

Wovoka looked around himself once more. "But what is this place? Why have I been brought here?"

"You must answer that, Wovoka. Look around you. Is there something that drew you here?"

He took his time, carefully searching the room. The squat, white box was filled with blue fire, rising up when he turned the handle. The tall box was opened to reveal a lighted, cool storehouse of food, enough to feed several families. There were paintings of green hills on the walls, paintings of his brothers dancing in the firelight.

There was a window. Wovoka looked out, not at the barren pasture but at many small dwellings full of light. There was peace here. Families gathered for their nightly meal.

"The buffalo?" he asked eagerly, trying not to appear disrespectful.

The old man smiled. "Buffalo? Yes, there are many buffalo."

"There must be dancing and singing!" Wovoka rejoiced.

"Only four days a month," the old man replied. "We always wear one feather to tell who we are."

Wovoka gripped his head. The pain was returning.

"And the white man?" he asked but the old man was dissolving, becoming unreal. His words to Wovoka were incomprehensible, and the pain forced him to his knees. He reached out, not wanting to leave this perfect otherworld and trying to remember everything the Great Spirit had told him.

When he woke, he was shivering on the cold, hard floor. The streaming daylight was full of dust motes on his bare walls. He was back.

He contemplated what he had heard, what he had seen. The cold water of the lake was welcome on his hot face. The moldy crust of bread that he must eat made him yearn to look in the tall, cold, food box in that other place.

Had he dreamed, like the white man, first of demons

then of saviors? How would he know what to tell his brothers of the Great Spirit's word? He was confused and angry.

"How will I know?" he questioned the sky aloud.

He must be mad. Wovoka glanced up at the face of the sun again. Something seemed to be devouring it. His eyes burned. Slowly, the sun disappeared, a blackness falling on the land—a shadow.

And he knew what he must say, what he must do. The Great Spirit had told him how to reach that other world. He must not fail.

The world was dark then, the face of the sun covered by the black shadow. Wovoka swore to tell his brothers.

As quickly, the shadow passed. The sun warmed the earth. And the people began to speak of miracles and a medicine man from the plains.

The dancers have been dancing for hours. Through the long night they shout and sing. The fire is kept strong, burning away the darkness. A dancer falls to the ground, exhausted, hoarse. Another comes to take his place.

Stories had begun to filter down through the tribes. The white man hates the Ghost Dance. He will use it for his revenge.

Wovoka believed at first that the Great Spirit would protect them. Then he tried to believe that it was a test, a way of measuring their courage. Paiute, Sioux, Cheyenne, Arapaho, Kiowo, Shoshone—they would continue to dance.

The Ghost Dance grows like fire to dry kindling. They have been rescued from their despair and misery by the words of the prophet Wovoka. The new world is coming.

Silently, he watches the faces of the dancers. In his heart, fear has come to rest.

Just that morning, Wovoka had word from the northern territories. The white man had found a way to strike at their heart. Aging Sioux Chief Sitting Bull had been murdered along with two hundred men, women, and children at Wounded Knee, South Dakota.

Wovoka's brothers stood unbelieving. In their eyes was hatred, blood in their mouths for revenge. There was no more dancing, no song. The new world had been forgotten.

Why had this happened? The Great Spirit wished to test them. This rang hollow. The Prophet could no longer say these words. Wovoka could find no heart to speak with his brothers, to plead with them to keep dancing.

In the almost two years since he had his vision of the Great Spirit, Wovoka had not seen him again. He had begun to doubt his presence.

He walks the mountain trails at night, searching. More of his brothers have died. There is talk of killing around the cold ashes of the Ghost Dance fires.

Wovoka stares at the black sky then down at the quiet valley. The pain, when it comes, is welcome. His knees buckle, but he stands straight. His thin frame is racked by chills.

Then the pain is gone. He looks at the strange, smoking coaches that white men with their noisy children race from. There is light in the clearing and the sound of singing. Cautiously, he edges closer.

The men are dancing. Their bodies are well fed in their feathers and paint. Some are standing outside the circle wearing one feather, small papers on their shirts with white man's writing he cannot read. A young girl with long, black braids sells cups of liquid to the children.

A loud voice that seems to echo around him welcomes them to the show. White men begin to clap their hands as they sit in a circle on the ground around the dancers. There are buffalo, many buffalo. They stand carved and lifeless on a table. Beside them are colored beads and feathers. Music begins to play.

Wovoka turns away. A great wind bears him upward. He lifts his arms to the Great Spirit, the Mother, and begs to be taken away.

He awakes, and his body is cold and stiff on the

mountain ridge. It feels heavy and awkward around him. He struggles to open his eyes.

An eagle flies by, his sharp eyes pierce Wovoka's soul. The eagle carries the single white feather from Wovoka's hair in his clutch. The Great Spirit has sent his messenger to carry away his dream.

In Wovoka's hand is a wooden buffalo with painted eyes.

The men are dancing. But only in the silence of one man's heart.

Wovoka the man finally awakes on his pallet. The room is cold. The floor is hard beneath him. There are dry leaves rustling through his mind as he recalls the dream.

He could feel the beat of the men's hearts as they danced, smell the sweat of their bodies. They had been as real as the cold in his joints or the tears in his eyes.

Day is coming. And with it, a shadow that will surely pass over the sun.

He will go to find his brothers and teach them the Ghost Dance. For a time, at least, there would be hope again. And laughter. His brothers would remember his name.

Wovoka, the prophet, steps into the morning. He pushes the painted buffalo into his pocket.

It is good.

GHOST DANCE SONG
I come to tell news
I come to tell news
The buffaloes are coming again
The buffaloes are coming again
My father tells.
The Dead People are coming again
The Dead People are coming again
My father tells
The earth will be made new
The earth will be made new

Says the Mother

Assassin

Some stories start with characters, some with plot, some with just a hint of an idea. "Assassin" actually came about with the plot twist, and we worked our way out from there, asking each other questions like who was involved, how the events of the story came about, and when and where it took place. When we came up with Emma, we knew we had it.

Had she been wrong?

Emma kept her eyes focused on the high tower, a stark skeleton against the gray sky. There was no light, no sign of movement. It had rained recently, and the acrid smell of moisture clung to the air, dripping down the long sides of the empty buildings to the ground.

The city was small but densely populated. Level on level of worker's hives and entertainment complexes competed with living quarters and the intercity transport systems. A black mist clung to everything. The street squelched with layers of black debris.

In the tiny side street, no more than a path, she kept her vigil through the rain and the soot. The skulking of animal feet in the unseen scraps of trash brought only a faint twitch to her cheek. She dared not move. Her breathing was quick and shallow, afraid that any movement might be detectable, even in the darkness. Stray drops of moisture slid silently down her back from the short cap of her dark hair. She quelled the shiver it produced and kept her eyes skyward. It wasn't possible that she could have missed him. He was good, but she was better. Emma knew him, knew his movements, his habits. While he went about his business, not realizing, she had come to know him. While he traveled from world to world, she had watched and waited for this day. When he finished his kill tonight, it would be his last. He hadn't noticed her and wouldn't see her, until it was too late.

She allowed herself the briefest smile at the thought and stilled her impatience and her trembling hands. There was time. She had come this far. She could wait a little longer.

* * *

"Can you see her?"

"No," he responded tightly. "But I know she's there. She's tracked his moves for five years. She doesn't get impatient."

"How can you be sure it's tonight? This could be another grid point for her."

The older, heavier man stood and stretched himself carefully, mindful of old injuries that ached in the damp, night air. The thin walls of the tiny apartment kept out little weather and less sound, but it was a perfect overlook. The street far below was too dark to penetrate without assistance.

The younger man seated at the window wore the night visor. His body was held rigidly, and his gaze never wavered.

"Those things give me a headache," his partner volunteered after a moment when the other man continued to stare down at the street. "She's crazy, you know. She has to be."

"Just dedicated," his partner disagreed quietly. "And damn good at it."

"Maybe we should ask her to join us." The other man snorted. "Hey, crazy lady. Let us help you kill the bad man that murdered your daddy."

"Don't laugh. She might just beat us to him."

"And this damned city might just grow flowers."

The younger man removed his visor and ran his hand over his tired eyes. They had been there, watching her, for two days. She'd been crouched in the street. There were no words for that sort of devotion to hatred. It fascinated and repelled him, just as Emma did.

"I don't think he's gonna show."

"She hasn't been wrong yet in the last two years. Every time he's killed, she was there beforehand. She knows he's coming. She can sense it."

"Oh, great. Now she's a damn mind jumper! She might just be lucky, you know."

"Then let's hope she's lucky tonight."

"And that she doesn't mind us making off with the man she wants to kill, right? You know, we might have to take her out if she's as damned obsessed as you think."

"We'll deal with that when we have to. Just be ready to move."

"This woman's crazy, man." The older man wheezed as he laughed. "She wants his blood. Or whatever it is that runs through him."

The man resumed his vigil at the window.

* * *

Emma was exhausted. If she stood, she wasn't sure her legs would hold her. She'd lost feeling in them a long time before.

How long had she been there? A terrible giddiness seized her. Really, how long? In this dirty alley or another. On Parsis 3, when he'd killed the Senate Leader. Or the year before when she'd waited, a stark thrill clenching her throat closed when she saw him. He'd killed a prominent businessman on that world.

The kills were duly noted, times and places carefully plotted. It made a graph that covered the lower half of the known systems and represented blood and death. And all of her adult life.

She tasted blood in her mouth, biting hard until the

dizziness and nausea passed. Her eyes burned. They were full of sky and soot. The night would end with his death.

Or hers.

It was the culmination of every day since her father's death five years ago.

Emma felt for the cold, hard weapon with one hand. She knew its contours as well as she knew the lines of her own face. Handmade, precise to a millisecond of accuracy, it was a weapon she'd discovered in an obscure shop in old town Brigham, an ancient pirate's weapon, its handle lovingly smoothed with time and use.

It wouldn't matter where she hit him. Death would be long, slow, and painful beyond any death that could be inflicted by modern weapons. They were too quick, too clean. She wanted to see him die. She wanted to see him suffer, and she wanted to ask him why.

In all her travels, for all her understanding of him and his work, she still didn't understand where her father fit his pattern. This man, this assassin, murdered players—important political figures, heads of crime gangs, those who understood the rules. It wasn't that assassination was uncommon. It was a sure way to deal with rivals, an accepted way to play the game.

But her father had been a schoolteacher. They had lived just outside the original Mars colony of New Philadelphia since she'd been born. He'd been a gentle, learned man, full of art and poetry. But Daniel Fox hadn't been anyone of any importance.

Except to the young woman who'd turned at his side to see the black phantom of death swoop down to take his life.

He had been a graceful whisper, his movements economical and precise, like a carefully choreographed dance. Daniel Fox had been dead in an instant. There'd been no weapon but the assassin's hand.

Her father's body had jerked to the ground at her feet. Emma had looked up into the killer's face. It was passive and terrible, a nightmare she'd relived over and over, the scream gurgling in her throat, wondering if he would kill her as well. It had seemed to her that she had lost herself in the deep emptiness of his eyes. She'd faltered, reached out a hand to touch him, and he'd been gone. She could never say afterward what color his eyes were or if he was old or young. To her shame, she could recall asking him to take her with him and then crying when he had left her there alone. She couldn't recall what had possessed her to ask that of the man who had just killed her father. And now it had ceased to matter to her.

All that mattered was the black form stealthily sliding up the building.

She watched him in fascination. The winds at the top of that grotesque tower should have ripped him from the peak. But like a spider, he climbed slowly, carefully. There was never a movement out of place or a hint of sound. He never carried a weapon. She had recorded his kills over a hundred times. His victim would be dead in less than five minutes.

Except that this victim was not where the assassin was expecting him. John Maddox, the head of a striking miner's guild, had been scheduled for the corner suite on the tenth floor. Emma had changed those plans. Posing as a managing assistant, she had swept Maddox and his entourage of bodyguards to another floor at the back of the building. Overlooking the crowded transport deck, it wasn't a spot anyone with any clout would stay.

Fumbling at first, struggling to move her numbed body, Emma started down the alley as he disappeared into the building.

* * *

The two men in the overlooking window threw off their lethargy and stumbled to the door. The older man adjusted his weapon as he blinked in the light. "She's moving. He must be here."

"Stun," his partner reminded him. "We don't want either

of them dead."

"Right," the other man responded sarcastically but rotated his weapon for the proper setting. He followed his partner down the dimly lit corridor, mumbling and pulling at his filthy collar.

The commotion in the front entrance was short but noisy. Several inebriated customers were leaving the lounge area when the two deputies entered, confronting the hotel workers and demanding to wake the manager.

"I don't understand. What do you mean someone is going to be killed?" a short dark-skinned man pressed forward, one shoe missing. "What's going on?"

"We need to see your registration. Now."

"And I need to see your—"

"ID? Deputy Pat Lacy." The younger man pulled out his holo-badge. "My partner, Deputy Bob Seaforth."

"I'll have to find the registration tape."

"Quickly," Pat urged. "There isn't time."

* * *

Emma knew her timing must be perfect. When the assassin found his prey had gone, she was certain that he would leave the building and plot another time to make the kill. He would want to make his exit clean and fast. The turbo lift was down for repair, so the stairs were his only escape. He never left a kill the way he went in. He would find her waiting for him.

She used the ID card she'd forged to gain entrance to the service area, ignoring the looks she received from the workers on duty. There was a service lift that only went to the eighth floor. She would wait for him there.

He would be faster than her, coming down the stairs like a black wraith. But there was only one entrance to the service lift and only one exit. He would know of its existence, even as she did. It would be the fastest way out.

Emma waited on one side of the opening as she reached the eighth floor. There was no sign of him there, but it could only be seconds. She pulled her weapon from beneath her jacket, icy fingers on the trigger. Each sense was alive to every nuance in the empty corridor. She pressed herself against the wall and tried to catch her breath.

Precious time went by—seconds on her lighted watch dial, hours in her thoughts.

Where was he? He was faster than that, faster than she should have been getting there.

It was too long. She rethought her moves, plotted where his steps could have taken him. He might have decided not to use the service lift. He might have considered the risk of being seen too great.

Or he might have learned about Maddox's move to the fifth floor. Emma's heart stopped.

The door was open from the corridor. It was only a crack, but it was enough to tell her that he was there. Emma swore beneath her breath, recklessly pushing inside and shutting the door behind her.

It was going to be there and then. She wouldn't let him cheat her of that night.

There was no sound in the two huge, connecting rooms, except for the slight snoring and gasping of the sleeping forms around her. Faint light filtered in from the greasy window that faced her. Death was somewhere close at hand.

Emma waited as her eyes adjusted to the darkness. There seemed to be nothing out of place. The Maddox group was large and slept in every available space from chairs to desktops. They were sprawled across the floor. Carefully she picked her way around their bodies. Her head thrummed with tension, and the hand with the weapon was nearly humming as she listened for any slight sound out of the ordinary.

The two rooms were arranged so that one could be used for sleeping, one for entertaining. Only the second, the smaller room had a bed. Maddox would have that room.

The door was open. A form sprawled across the threshold, rolling over slightly as she passed over the top of the man. He mumbled something unintelligible in his sleep then was still.

Emma took a shadow of a breath and moved into the bedroom. There were no windows. Its closeness was suffocating, as twenty men slept around Maddox. A thread of light picked up his round form on the bed beneath the heavy blankets. There was no other way. She had to move closer and edge up next to him.

She stepped carefully over another man on the floor then climbed slowly on the bed and shifted so that the small particle of light could reach from behind her to Maddox's sleeping form. Ready to fire at the faintest sound, she held her weapon tightly before her. Her knee creased the blanket next to Maddox's shoulder, and his head rolled limply toward her, eyes wide and empty in the fractured light.

Emma ground her teeth in despair at the face of the dead man. A shadow flitted from the corner of her eye at the threshold where the sleeping man had been. The threshold was empty.

She had crossed over the top of him as he pretended to be asleep.

Enraged, she choked back a scream of hatred, springing for the doorway. On the deck far below, the transport had pulled in, the station lights flaring upward. Crowds of workers streamed out to the platform, noisily jostling for empty spaces on the ramp to the street.

He was there in the doorway, going out of the room to the corridor—slender, tall, and pure black as she was sure his heart had to be. He paused, turned his head, and looked at her. Emma, knowing she would never have a better chance, fired her weapon. It missed him wildly, but she saw his body turn toward her. In an instant, he would be on her. Her knife flashed in the light as she hurled it across the room. There was no sound, but she knew the blade had found him.

But he was gone. The noise from the platform roused the sleeping men in the room. From the corridor, she heard the sound of running footsteps. Someone shouted, and another voice replied.

He hadn't had time to kill her. But she was still trapped in the room with Maddox dead and his men starting to move clumsily around her. They would think she was the murderer unless she could escape.

A man ran by the room in the corridor, obviously following the black ghost she'd nearly caught in the act. A second man followed more slowly, firing his weapon past the first man.

"What the—" a husky voice began as a large hand clamped on her shoulder.

Emma moved instinctively, using her gun as a weapon to free herself. She hit the man hard but didn't stop to watch his reaction. Like a wraith herself, she was out of the room and into the corridor.

* * *

They never had a chance of catching him. Pat's chest heaved with exertion of climbing endless flights of stairs. Bob caught up with him at the end of the hall, falling to his knees as he fought to breathe and dropped his weapon.

"Was that him? Where did he go?"

"I don't know. He's gone."

"What about the woman?" Bob grunted, slamming his fist into the black wall. "Where's the damn woman?"

Pat looked up, seeing Emma's retreating figure as she reached the stairs and was gone. "Maddox must be dead."

Bob laughed. "Tell me again how good she is. Tell me how she's gonna lead us to him and we'll get the credits for him."

Loud voices came from the Maddox suite. A man stumbled from the room, calling for someone to find the police.

Pat shook his head and holstered his weapon as he pictured her thin, pale face. "There'll be another time. He doesn't wait long between kills. And she's always there."

* * *

Her escape route already planned, Emma quickly slipped into the crowd at the transport deck. The citywide tube train ran quickly and silently through the dark streets, people packed within its rounded hull until there was no room for movement.

She was glad for the press of flesh against her own. There was no more energy left to hold her upright and no strength to consider her next move or the fact that her plan, so carefully mastered, had failed. She would need time to recover. It would take long hours to research his next possible kill.

Three days before, she had found a small, cheap room in a lower level of the city. It was cold and dirty, but no one bothered to ask her name or what she was doing there. There was a single light in the center of the wall, a cracked phoso lamp that radiated a weird, green glow. The price of the room didn't include a window.

She leaned her head against the wall. There was a welling in her to see an ocean, a real ocean with the sight and smell of salty air and water.

A frisson of awareness rather than sound shivered up her spine. She turned, dropping to the floor as she moved. Her knife cracked the plastic lamp case, splintering the glowing beam like a kaleidoscope. The door closed, and she was smoothly trapped.

"I was returning your toy," a husky silvered voice whispered. "You should be more careful where you leave it."

Emma stayed where she was, calculating the space between them. His back was to the door, his face shadowed. She could feel his gaze on her.

"What do you want me to say?" she hissed. "I hope it hurt. I'm sorry you aren't dead. Kill me and be damned."

He laughed—or at least the low, rasping sound seemed to be laughter. "You wanted my attention. You have it."

"I wanted your death. Slow and painful. I wanted to hear

you beg." Her weapon was just out of reach near the bed port under the light. If she could manage to stretch forward—

"Emma Fox, you've spent your whole adult life following me. Isn't there something else you wanted to say? Don't you want to know the truth?"

"The truth?" she scoffed. "The truth is you murder people. You murdered my father like you murdered Maddox tonight. And you're very good at it."

"And you're very good at finding me. You led those deputies to me. All they had to do was watch you."

"If you knew that," she asked, eyes narrowing, trying to see his face, "why didn't you kill me before now?"

"I haven't come to kill you. If I had, we wouldn't be having this conversation."

"Then what do you want from me?" She moved a fraction closer to the side of the wall.

"I've come to tell you a story."

Emma made her move, grabbing the gun. She swung it toward him without further thought. The firing mechanism jammed but not before she saw that he had moved as well.

She felt the pressure and pain on her wrist before she saw him. The gun clattered uselessly to the floor. "Kill me. Or leave me. I can't sit in the same room with you and let you live."

"Your choice of weapons leaves me aghast with admiration. The agony of its death is terrible to watch. But for speed, you would have been better off with something less creative." He moved away from her, tossing the weapon on the bed port. "You will listen to what I have to say without any other attempts at my life or yours. Or I will bind you and tape your mouth shut, and then you will listen."

Emma sat up wearily, her back to the wall. "Say it and get out."

His sigh was audible. His face turned away from the fractured light. "Years ago, two men persuaded the central government to fund a research project that promised to do away with a large, expensive portion of security in their system. They proposed a way to clone an animate creature that could seek out any life form whose genetic coding was induced into its creation. A single hair or drop of blood and there was no way to stop the creature from finding its prey. The hunter and the hunted became as one until the lifeform was found, the creature destroyed, and another created for a new fugitive."

"I do live in this system," she retorted. "I've read about the Van de Scheer process and the work they've done bringing in murderers like you. Of course, they couldn't bring you in, could they? Since no one seems to know who you are, and they need something to clone the creature."

"Karl Van de Scheer became famous as the father of the process, but he had a partner—Daniel Fox."

"What?" Her mouth went dry.

"He dropped away from the project because of disagreements between partners. What Van de Scheer didn't know was that Fox dropped out to create a creature of his own that would seek out and destroy his partner. He believed the project had been mostly his own work and that Van de Scheer had stolen his fame."

"Liar. You're lying!" Emma clenched her fists.

The shadow's voice stayed even, despite her outburst. "Daniel Fox created his creature. Soulless, mindless, except for one thing. Killing Karl Van de Scheer. But when Van de Scheer was dead, Fox panicked and fled off-world, leaving behind the creature that should have been destroyed when his only reason to live was over."

"I've seen a Van de Scheer creature," she rasped. "They're small, almost shapeless..."

"No one thought about their survival past that stage. They were never supposed to live longer than it took to find their prey."

"My father would never—"

He grasped her roughly by the arms, pulling her to her

feet. "He was not your father."

Emma struggled with him. His strength was overwhelming, but she succeeded in pushing him back against the wall, knocking them both off balance. He held them both near the light, bringing their faces close together. "Look at me," he commanded. "And remember what you see."

In the green light, his features were even more complex—intelligent eyes, colorless because of the radiant source, high cheekbones, and a chin made slightly too sharp. Emma had attended school. She knew the faces of the heroes extolled by the government. It was so like the face of Karl Van de Scheer, dead long before she was born.

"You're—"

"I was created from some of his genetics, not all. I am not Karl Van de Scheer. Or Daniel Fox, though I claim genetics from each." He pushed her back toward the bed port. "I don't have a name. I do, you will admit, have a vocation."

"You murdered Daniel Fox."

He kept his eyes on her as he spoke. "Before he had a chance to finish his work on his new creature."

"Which would have been created to destroy you?"

"Only if he had finished the genetic coding process."

Emma was instantly on her feet. "You might look like Van de Scheer, but you're insane. The killing has destroyed your mind. I knew Daniel Fox. I loved him. He was incapable of what you're saying. Why are you telling me this?"

He laughed and shook his head. "Think about it. I've told you the truth. Try to remember everything you can about your childhood with Fox. Take your knife to the Van de Scheer Institute. The answers are your answers as well."

"I don't know what you mean." She stalled while she reached behind herself for the knife, still stuck in the padded wall. She didn't want to hear his explanations. Blade in hand, she turned to face him.

Emma glanced around herself. She was alone. The door was tightly closed. She checked her weapon. It would need refitting, but he hadn't damaged it permanently. The knife in the wall light was hers. The sticky blood was his.

Quickly, she deposited the knife into a disposable bag and sealed it carefully. She would follow his suggestion and go to the Van de Scheer Institute. But he might be surprised when she was done. With a sample of his blood, she could have a creature cloned that would hunt him down no matter where he hid or where he sought his prey. He was a lying murderer, and she wouldn't let the questions he'd raised make her forget what he'd done. She was her father's daughter.

It took Emma days of hard, grueling travel in whatever transport she could find to reach the Institute. She didn't mind the ache in her bones from being confined in cramped spaces or the hunger that gnawed in her belly during the long, empty hours. All she could think of was killing that thing that had killed her father.

She had no intention of allowing the Van de Scheer creature to kill that shadow. She would use the creature to track it down. Between them, they would hunt him to ground.

But she would kill him. She would watch the life ebb from his body as he had watched it run out of her father.

And then? She had no plans after that moment. Perhaps she would travel to some world that had an ocean. Hadn't she always wanted to see an ocean? She would sleep and eat.

And then? She cleared her mind. It was best not to think about then.

Emma was careful not to be followed again. She didn't need that complication. She had been so single-minded in following her prey that she hadn't realized that she might be attracting others who wanted to find him. She wouldn't let that happen.

It had to be her kill. Hadn't she lived for it? Hadn't it obsessed her for as long as she could remember?

The Van de Scheer creature didn't come cheap. Except in private use, the creature was only used as a last resort in tracking the worst of criminals. It was limited to those who could afford to pay for it, although that didn't stop its illegal usage. It was unparalleled in its deadly targeting, and it never failed.

Once or twice, she felt his presence. If he was following her, it wasn't actually detectable to her. Yet she knew he was there. Would he strike at the last moment before she could accomplish her goal? Or was he really as delusional as he'd sounded in her room that night?

Her father's account was large enough that she was received with open arms at the Institute. There was no last-minute attack, no attempt of any kind to stop her. Emma was puzzled. She would certainly have taken him. She shrugged it off. If he was insane enough to think she would see the light of truth in what he'd told her and spare his life, he was going to be deeply disappointed.

A tech was appointed to her. He explained the process of creation and destruction of the creature and that they would need DNA from both herself and her intended victim. Her victim's DNA would bond the creature to finding its prey. Her own would control it. Briefly, he outlined the risk that the creature could become confused and stalk the donor rather than the prey. It was unlikely, but they had a remedy. Emma would be given a signal that would kill the creature. Then they could start over.

While they spoke, DNA was drawn from her. She surrendered the knife with his blood on it. Both were loaded into the computer that would begin the creation process. Emma filled out forms, transferred credits, and waited impatiently for the process to continue.

A red light blinked on the control panel, and the tech blinked with it. He smiled. "Excuse me, please."

He left her there in the tiny cubicle, and the door slid closed behind her. There was no sound except for the slight hum of the machinery. The light was subdued. She tapped her fingers on the tabletop until the door slid open again with a faint rasping sound.

"There's been some mistake," the tech explained with an apologetic air. "We'll have to sample your DNA again. Sorry."

She sat still while the process commenced. "What's the problem?"

"No problem," the tech explained while the results went back to the computer. The red light blinked again. The tech swallowed hard and excused himself again.

When he returned, he wasn't alone. An older man, obviously his superior, came with him. They both looked at her curiously. In turn, Emma stared back at them.

"The DNA on the knife is the same as your own DNA," the tech explained in a squeaky voice. "You must have accidentally—"

"No!" she protested. "The blood on that knife is from the man I want killed."

"You've made a mistake," the older man assured her. "The DNA on that knife is specifically the same as your own. You must have tainted the sample with your own. You'll have to get another sample. Unless you want the creature to find you."

Emma glared at them. "One more test. And I want to see the results."

The supervisor nodded. The tech nervously did the test again.

When it was finished, the red light blinked again. Emma wanted to smash that light. The supervisor pulled up a small screen to show her the results.

"The DNA is very specific. This couldn't even be the DNA from a close relative. This is your DNA. Unless you and the person you want killed were both created from the same source." He chuckled richly and put down the screen. "We'll have to charge you for those tests. Then you'll have to get a fresh sample."

Emma was stunned. The knife had not even nicked her skin. That had to be his blood. She stared at their impassive faces then mumbled something unintelligible and walked out of the Institute.

Her mind shut down. She wandered around the docking stations until she found a freighter that would take her somewhere—anywhere. She needed time to think. It was a trick of some kind. He had manipulated the blood on the knife.

But how had he made it her blood?

Ensconced in another tiny, dark, almost airless cell on the huge freighter, she closed her eyes. The freighter pulled away from the docking mechanism, with deep groans and sighs as it started on its long voyage.

"Now you know the truth," he whispered.

"And what is that?" she asked without moving or opening her eyes, not at all surprised that he had managed to find her.

"We are the same."

Emma was silent. The words refused to register in her brain.

"He made you to kill me. He just reversed the sequence. Once Van de Scheer was gone, he could use his DNA freely to program my assassin. You, Emma."

"Then why aren't you dead?"

"Because I killed him before he could finish the sequencing." The quality of his voice changed to something undefinable. "You were not fully programmed to do anything but find me."

"So now I've found you." She took a deep, trembling breath. "And I can't kill you. What does that leave me?"

"Life," he countered. "There is no one to destroy you since Fox is gone. In the universe, we are the same, and yet we are alone."

She sat up slowly and looked at him. He was perched on

the edge of the narrow bed port. He was not a shadow but was the form and substance of all she could remember, everything that she had dreamed.

Emma realized the truth of his words—how she had been deceived and they had been separated. How she had very nearly killed the only one in the universe like herself.

A tear slipped down her cheek, and she waited without breathing as he reached out his hand and touched her face. She shivered.

"We are one." He took her hand and pressed it to his, their supple fingers meshing.

"One," she repeated.

He brought his mouth gently to hers, barely touching the contour of her lips. She gazed into his eyes, so like her own. Their breath mingled. Their hearts beat together to the same rhythm.

"And then?" she asked the question she had dreaded when she had thought of his death.

"And then I shall take you to a world that is only the sea and the sand and the suns. I long to find the sea. And then we will live our own lives and not those decided or created for us."

Emma settled against him, finding a peculiar kind of peace with him that she had never known without him. Daniel Fox had created them, but he had not been able to destroy them. She smiled against his skin. "I feel a different urge, suddenly, but it's no less strong than the urge to kill you."

He lay full-length beside her, fluid and strong. "Then let us find a direction for that urge, my love. And then..."

The Courtship

The American South is full of wise women, healers, and witches. While it takes place in the world of the Retired Witches series, this story shows that not all of them need spellbooks or familiars. The Geechee and other low-country witches use roots and herbs, and sometimes, they may even be touched by deeper, more powerful forces.

It would come during the first two weeks of October. Just like Nan said when I was fifteen and a drop of red slipped down my thigh. She haloed me then and told me what she saw in those colors flashing around my head. It would always be in the fall for me, even though I was a child of the spring.

"It won't be easy, your life," she told me, those big, clever hands laying on my head. "You'll wait and then some."

Nan had raised five babies with those hands and buried two. Her gift was music. She could play anything to tune from a hand saw to a fiddle. She could make jam bubbling on the stove sound sweet, and there was no denying it.

But Nan was dead three years before that first October came for me.

I was twenty and thought myself handsome in a dark, round-hipped fashion. I spent hours in front of the polished stove front, pursing my lips, dreaming of the gift I had yet to receive.

"You look like a fool," my sister, Myrtle, told me, catching me at my favorite pastime.

"Jealous?" I raised a practiced brow at her.

"Grow up, Letty." She stirred the stew on the stove. "And make yourself useful for once. Get some water from the well."

I took the pitcher from the table and smiled at her, knowing it made me look like a cat.

"You know Mama says I don't need to do nothin' till my gift comes," I reminded her, telling her in my unsubtle way that I was doing her a favor.

"Maybe you got no gift comin'," she taunted me, her plain face sly and mean. "I think it just passed you by."

I wanted to slam the door as I left her, but I knew it would give her pleasure. I just smiled again, my apricot smile, sweet and juicy, and sauntered outside.

It was mild yet. The weather hadn't turned, but there was something different about that October. It was a smell in the air, a feeling in my bones as I walked to the well in front of the house. Leaves were falling all around me, crunching under my bare feet.

I put down the pitcher on the corner of the well and started to raise the bucket. I was thinking thoughts as deep and full as the water in the stone circle. The birds were singing, flies droning in the sunlight.

Then, suddenly, I was standing in the shadow of a cloud. The air grew cold and still. No sound touched that silence. No breath of wind moved in the trees.

A whirlwind of leaves started up from the ground, and the biggest tree around me trembled, leaves spewing down, red and gold, in a shower over me till I was near choked with them.

I've come.

I looked around at that sky-bound tornado of leaves, and I was scared all right. But I was young and full of myself.

"I don't know who you are," I told that cold, flat voice, "but you can just go back where you come from."

I've come. For you.

It took my breath away, the power in that voice, just those few words. I could feel my heart beating, almost bursting from my chest. Leaves tangled in my hair and my skirt, wrapped themselves close to me as my own skin.

"No!" It was the only word in my head, ripped from me, my breath turning white in the frozen air. I repeated it again, more aware of what I had said, stamping my leaf-covered foot as I spoke.

The whirlwind roared faster till I thought I would be deaf with the sound. Then, just as sudden, it was gone.

The leaves floated gracefully down to the ground, and the sun shone again. The earthenware pitcher on the side of the well had cracked, and the water in the bucket had frozen.

Myrtle screamed from the house, and I left it there, running back through the new blanket of leaves on the ground.

That October took my mama. Myrtle just looked at me. We never talked about it later, but she knew, and she blamed me for Mama's death. I pursed my lips and looked away. I wasn't ready to go yet.

It wasn't long after that the people started coming to me. I could look at them and tell what was wrong, and I knew just what to do for it. They started calling me a healer after a few years passed. Every day, season after season, they came to me, and I took care of them. Some said they had a dream that brought them. Some didn't say, just stared at me, scared-like.

When I was thirty-five, it came again.

I had just finished treating a young man from town. He drove his shiny, red sports car a hundred miles to see me.

He was dying. I could see it in his eyes. He could see it in mine that I couldn't help him. The darkness seeped through him, but there wasn't a plant or powder that could stop it. I gave him something for the pain. He smiled in a way that made me think it wouldn't be long, and I watched him drive away.

The sky was so blue that it hurt my eyes to look at it. The sunshine made me think about my mama. I was sitting on the front porch, and I could hear Myrtle singing in the kitchen. She reminded me of Mama, always taking care of everyone around her.

"Marry him," she had told me one hot summer night the year before.

I was shelling beans with her on the porch, crickets chirping in the dark around us. Johnney, dark Johnney Amblen, had asked me to be his wife. He was a good man, big and fine and strong. He would take care of a woman. When he looked at me, I knew he loved me.

"I can't," I answered, knowing it caused her pain.

"He'd make you a fine husband." She sighed.

I didn't have to look up and see her face in the porch light to know that Myrtle loved Johnney Amblen, that it was her she wanted him to take care of, not me.

"I don't love him," I said, guilty feeling even though I couldn't help Johnney loved me.

"Might stop it happening again," she pointed out, always sensible.

"Might," I had agreed back in July.

I sat on those same steps in October, with that cold wind coming up from the woods and tried to wonder if it might have kept it away.

But it was too late. I could see it coming straight up the path, blowing leaves and dirt before it like the devil's own breath. It stopped in front of me where I sat, fifteen years later, not so scared.

I've come.

"Why?" It was the question that I'd wished I'd asked before. I'd thought it a thousand times since that first time it had come.

For you.

A leaf spun around, danced across the air, and caressed my cheek, before sliding into my lap.

"You killed my Mama."

A dozen leaves, red and gold, spun up in a single line straight for the sky. They caught fire as they went up higher, bursting as I watched, burning in that hot, blue October sky.

I've come for you now.

I looked at the leaf in my lap. It caught fire, and I jumped up, patting at my skirt to put out the fire it made there.

"No," I said again, facing the leaves that had begun to blow up from the ground. "I won't go with you. And this time, you leave what's mine alone, you hear?"

I thought all the dirt would be blown off the ground as it left. It moved through the underbrush, burning as it went, taking down hundred-year-old oak trees like they were twigs, turning the pond to steam.

People said something angry passed through that day. A storm shook the ground so hard it cracked and nothing ever grew there again. Hay burned where it lay in the fields. The smell of scorched earth was everywhere for weeks.

"What was that, Letty?" Myrtle asked, coming out of the house, wiping her hands on her apron.

I sat back down on the stairs. Lightning forked from the ground to the sky, and I shuddered.

"Looks like a storm," she answered herself, squinting off at the sky. "Best come in for supper."

I followed her inside, closing the door on the loud thunder that screamed like a voice in pain.

Myrtle died a few years later. I buried her next to Mama in the little churchyard, even though Reverend Taylor called us witches and said that it was blasphemy.

Years slipped away, rain and sun, summer and winter. I

healed folks that came to me. Sometimes I thought about Johnney Amblen in the night when the house was dark and I was alone. He'd married Mary Taylor, the Reverend's daughter, and died, working his farm, with his six fine sons around him.

I don't know exactly when I noticed that people weren't coming so much. I looked at my hands, all knotted and drawn, and knew they wouldn't be coming ever again.

One day, the end of September, I looked at my face in the rain-soaked window pane. I smiled my best cat smile.

But it made my face break down into years of lines, made my pretty, dark eyes look like raisins. My hair was still long and thick but the gray of the old cookstove instead of the black of coal.

I saw old Nan again in a dream the first night of October. In the morning, a single red leaf had blown in through the open window. It rested on the pillow near my cheek. I sniffed the air, and I knew he was coming back for me.

It had been so long that I had begun to think I had dreamed it. Geese flew by, noisy, overhead in the first clear light of dawn, heading away from the cold that was surely coming. I walked slowly down the stairs, the wood creaking with my old bones in the cool October morning.

Already it was near time to start up the wood heater. Mornings and nights were cold, frost had come early, spoiling some of the last harvest.

I boiled up some sassafras for tea and set two chipped china cups on the rough wooden table. There was summer honey from the meadow. The house smelled like the herbs drying from the ceiling. I wiped my hands on my old, white apron when a knock came at the door.

Fear and something near excitement made my hand shake when I opened it.

A carpet of leaves spread up the stairs and into the doorway. Two of them gracefully jumped to the table just beside the cups I'd set out.

I've come for you.

A golden leaf flew up, touched my hand, and dropped into my apron pocket. I turned back toward the stove and the tea that was brewing, picked up the pot, and poured the hot water into each cup. The smell of sassafras swirled through the kitchen.

"Maybe."

My eyes weren't so good, but I could make out the man coming up the path from the woods, the gnarled, wooden cane under a big, knotted hand. The strides weren't so long as they might once have been. I knew him at once, and my heart swelled with it.

I sat back in my chair with my cup of tea, facing the door, and watched him come. Leaves danced at his feet and hair, cartwheeling crazily, trying to get his attention in the blue sky. They trembled at his slightest glance.

I waited, as Nan had told me I would, wondering what I would say, feeling my face grow warm.

"So. You know me then," he spoke, standing in the doorway.

"I think I will," I told him haughtily, "when we've had our tea."

"You have made me wait."

"And you'll wait a little longer," I didn't mind telling him. I smiled my best smile as he sat down and picked up his cup of tea.

I looked around the old house, feeling the weight of the long summers and the cold winters that had passed there. It wouldn't be so bad, not going through another winter there.

"I'm ready now," I told him, facing him.

He held out his hand, and I put mine in it. He felt like dry, brittle leaves, and his voice was like the autumn wind. I thought about old Nan and Mama and Myrtle and closed my eyes on the bright October sunlight coming in through the open doorway.

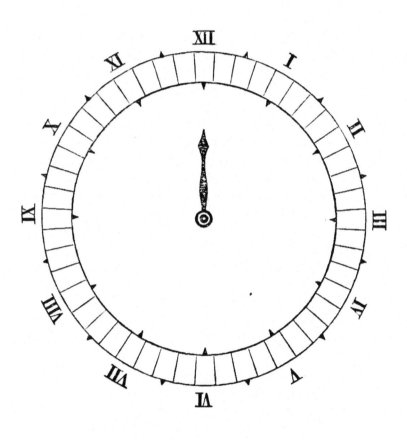

The Singing Trees of Jappa

When we were first married, we lived in a little A-frame house in the woods of northern Minnesota, a far cry from our home now in the piedmont of North Carolina. At times it felt so far from civilization, and we made friends with the plants and (some of) the animals who lived alongside us. As anyone who's spent any time in forests can tell you, sometimes the trees almost seem to sing. One day on a walk, we asked, what if the trees really were singing and we just didn't know how to hear them? The idea for this story was born then, but it was years before we put it on paper.

"Excuse me. That's my case—"

"Welcome to Jappa."

"Thanks." Fara nodded, amused as she accepted the flowered ceremonial welcome. Not so amused as her heavy case seemed to be moving further up the docking area.

"Welcome to Jappa."

"Thanks, uh, that's my case—"

"Our song is yours."

She looked down into the woman's smiling face beside her. "Excuse me but I do have to get—"

"Is there a problem, traveller?" A uniformed security officer, drab gray and stone faced, approached her. He was totally incongruous with the smiling, flower laden people around him.

Just as she was, Fara considered quickly, carefully choosing her next words. Jappa was outwardly the system's Mecca of culture and joy. Those flowers and smiles were sheathed in iron, however, when it came to the government.

"Welcome to Jappa," the sweet, sing song voice greeted everyone over the commotion. "Please disembark carefully. And remember, our song is yours."

When Fara's head came up again, there was a smile on her lips. "Thank you. There's no problem. I was... lost."

"Welcome to Jappa," a melodious male voice hailed her.

She turned eagerly away from the security guard's grim stare, took a breath, and willed his hand to move away from the communication device at his wrist.

"Our song is yours," the man smiled down at her, placing flowers around her neck.

Fara's smile died quickly. "What the—"

"Welcome." He smiled, putting an arm around her shoulder, effectively blocking them from the officer. "And smile."

She smiled and walked with him through the streaming throngs of people. "What the hell are you doing here?"

"Welcome to Jappa." He put flowers around an older woman's neck as she approached, smiling broadly. "I'm here to assist you, of course."

"Assist me by leaving at once, Commander. You lost your bid for violence here. I'll call when I need you."

"We brought your gizmo for you, Doctor. And we're here to safeguard your use of it."

Fara stopped dead. "Get off this planet until I have my chance, Commander or I'll—"

"You'll smile, Doctor, or we'll both end up explaining to the government why we're here."

She noticed the ring of security through the haze of her own anger. They discreetly elbowed through the crowd, occasionally stopping someone. She couldn't agree with his handling of the situation, not that she ever did, but she had to agree with his assessment.

"You'd better have authorization." She smiled, the words sliding from between clenched teeth. They resumed their path towards the lighted gateway. "And I need my case."

"I have both, Doctor," he assured her calmly. "Welcome to Jappa. Our song is yours."

It was little better than a field cruiser waiting for them at the gate. Fara's brown case and the woman who took it were both there.

"Get in, please," he urged. "We've wasted enough time. I'll explain on the way."

"Dr. Tucker, I'm Dabney," the woman said after a glance at the Commander. She inclined her close-cropped head slightly. "I'm your aide while you're here. If you need anything…"

"Thanks, Dabney." Fara climbed into the stripped down traveler carefully. "Why isn't another Echo officer here?"

"There were none available to come on such short notice." His tone was scathing in his unspoken opinion of her fellow officers. "You'll have to work with us."

"Commander Arlington." It was time to quit smiling and take control of what was supposed to be her project. "I want to see your authorization on this. We both know Central gave us thirty-six hours to try the device, and we both know how you feel about that decision."

"Technically, Doctor, we're on the same side, both the good guys, remember? We're here to save the Singing Trees. I'm aware of my job here. I hope you can say the same."

Fara ground her teeth. She'd worked with Matt Arlington before, and while he was very good at his job, he was incredibly difficult. Of course, his authorization was complete. She would have known he would never step over that line. The head of Central had put a red flag on the project when she'd checked. The extreme caution alert hadn't been there when she'd left Miccah station two days before.

"Possibly hostile government agents," Arlington explained, glancing over her shoulder at her contact disk. "Jappa's security chief seems to be expecting something. It's tighter than a Ullu's wart here. It could just be their own terrorist Ja Vir group."

"Ja Vir?"

"A group of terrorists... well, let's call them activists. Mostly singers and dancers who believe in trying to save the Last Forest. We think they're being led by Walt Borden."

"The composer?"

"Exactly. Their worst crime to date is distributing literature about the impending doom of Jappa. No more Singing Trees. No more wood to export. No more music."

"We can prevent that." Fara looked him in the eye.

"I could stop it right now," he countered.

"By disrupting the planet and destroying the government? The implications of that on the people of this planet—"

"Might be a little less happiness. I grant you, great music comes from this world. But they could use a dose of reality, Doctor. So could you."

"Reality is obviously what you make it, Commander Arlington." She sat back on the hard seat, watching as the vehicle progressed slowly through the heavy traffic. "The F 1 device works. This time tomorrow, we'll have accomplished the same goal but with no bloodshed and no disruption of normal planetary functions."

"Like last year on Delta 7's moon?"

She glared into his glacial green eyes. "We've both had our successes and failures, Commander. I'm sure you wouldn't want to repeat the entire record. And the discussion is pointless. Central verified the contract to Echo. That hasn't changed."

"As you say, Doctor." He shrugged, looking past her and into the street. "But we are here together under that same order. I have my command to follow. That includes keeping you and the F 1 device safe, seeing it installed and operational, and then taking the appropriate action."

Fara was silent, staring out at the city. Jappa's capital was alive with music and motion. The streets were filled with dancers in unbelievable colors. The air was rich with flowers and song. On every corner, a group of musicians played for the benefit of all who could listen. Unconsciously, she touched her hand to her ear.

"You aren't wearing the resonance deflector," Arlington told her, not at all shy at having seen the movement.

"There's no reason to, Commander."

"The resonance from the trees is what makes this planet famous, and you know how it affects the judgmental process—"

"Bringing a state of tranquility and well-being," she finished. "Yes, I know. The music of the Singing Trees."

"We can't afford those emotions in a potentially dangerous situation."

"My race lacks the necessary biological component to hear music or even feel the resonance from the trees."

"What do you hear?" he continued, despite her obvious distress.

"The words to a song… droning, in a way. There is no music on my home world." She leveled a cool gaze at him, daring him to pursue.

"So long as you aren't affected."

Fara turned back to the city, longing to hear as well as see the beauty of Jappa. It was a weakness, she supposed, that longing. It was also what drove her to bring her invention to save the music for everyone else. She wouldn't forget her plan. Or let Arlington bully her away from it.

Just outside the city, the road dropped away, becoming uneven and trenched. The graceful, low white structures that made up the city gave way to gold tipped grasses that sparkled with moisture in the sun. The wetlands stretched outward to the horizon, banking the distant glimpse of a formidable gray mountain range. Beyond those mountains were the dark green-black forests of Jappa.

"When the city ends, that's all there is." Arlington also looked toward the forests as the vehicle bounced through dry ruts.

"It's beautiful out here," she responded. "No one ever leaves the city?"

"Logging crews, mostly forced labor dredged from the prisons. Food is created artificially in the city. There are no industries except the wood export. Even that is simply harvested here. Craftsmen on six other planets create the stuff that makes everybody so happy."

"When you think that one hundred years ago, nothing was here, they haven't done so badly." Fara folded her hands in her lap to feign calm. "There was no way for them to know the wood's resonance would be so popular. Or that the trees were sterile and couldn't produce more."

"Not that it stopped them when they found out." It grated on him. Did she find the good side of everything? She wanted to save the universe from itself. People like that always scared him. They were dangerous. Especially the Echo enviro techs. They were too damn smart to be so gullible.

"I'm supposed to meet a forester at a shrine near the south point at the edge of the forest." She had decided to ignore his last remark. Just a few hours and she would have accomplished her goal. She could put up with his smug supremacy until then. "He's going to show me the area of trees that were determined to be the last that grew here. That's where the device needs to be."

"We can't just walk into the forest like tourists, you know. They have security everywhere. My group is at the east end of the forest. It's a good, defensible position."

"I'm sure it is, Commander. But I need that contact. I don't have time to search for the prime area myself."

"Doctor—"

"Commander," Dabney called out. "Checkpoint, sir."
Just ahead of the bend in the track was a waiting security
group. The width of the road was crossed by a primitive
electric fence to prevent blockade running.
"How many?"

"Looks to be about twenty, sir." Dabney adjusted her
field glasses after stopping the vehicle just inside the curve of
a large stand of grass.
"We'll take the skis from here, Lieutenant. You know
what to do." He reached behind the seat and dragged out a
large, flat oval that he tossed to Fara. "Aero ski, land
recognizance. Ever use one?"
"No." She studied the lightweight board as she juggled it
with her case and missed the look that passed between her
companions. "But haven't they already seen us?"
"They've seen the cruiser. Dabney knows what to do."
He got out of the vehicle and took Fara's ski from her before
heading into the tall grass.
"You can't mean to go through that alone?" Fara urged.
"Why don't you come with us?"
"As you said, they've seen the vehicle. If we aren't
down there shortly, they'll come here. I can throw them off
your track. When I crash through their barricade, that will
give you the time you need."
Fara looked at her earnest, young face. "Good luck, then,
Dabney."
"Doctor," the Commander growled from the grass.
As Fara left the cruiser, Dabney saluted them both. She
pushed the throttle high, whining the light engine, then
squealed off down the road in a cloud of dust.
"Will she be all right? Won't they put her in prison?"
"Dabney's tough. I trained her for this mission. We all
have our job to do, Doctor."
Fara shook her head at their lack of concern for life, all
life, one of the most basic differences between their two

groups. She loosened the strap on her case so it was able to go over her shoulder. "All right, Commander. What now?"

"Now we move." He pulled the handgrip lever from the top of the ski then locked it in place. "Simple and reliable. Steer with the grip directional. Start up and power down with the foot pedal. One speed. Try it."

From his tone, Fara could tell what he thought of the chance she'd be able to use the ski the first time. She stepped on the board and took the grip in both her hands, turning it experimentally. She shifted the case to her back and tapped the foot pedal. The aero ski glided, almost silently, across the damp ground. She maneuvered carefully between tall grass stalks, their height dwarfing her as she passed.

"Set your directional for east." Commander Arlington pulled alongside her. The narrow opening forced his ski almost on top of hers.

Shouts and weapon fire combined with the sound of vehicles starting, drawing their attention.

"Dabney," Fara said briefly, glad for the cover of the grass yet still uneasy over leaving the girl alone.

"She'll be fine, Doctor," he reprimanded. "Could I get some co op from you on this?"

She shook her head. "We need to go south."

"We check in with my team first, Doctor. Then we find your contact." He checked her protest. "It won't do you much good to find your contact without the F 1, will it?"

Fara pushed her case behind her for the second time since she'd climbed on the ski, the movement jerking a little to the right.

"Would you like me to take that for you?" he asked calmly. He had been expecting it, after all.

"It's fine," she replied confidently, almost stepping off the ski. "I can handle it."

He doubted it but didn't press her.

What had seemed effortless at the beginning of the trek quickly became a test of stamina. The skis were much better than walking but constantly had to be guided through the grass. The sun was nearing the mountains when Fara found herself fighting hard to stay alert and upright. They hadn't stopped for food or water since that morning. Commander Arlington had pressed a small nutri wafer into her hand what seemed like days before. She was starving and thirsty, and her back felt as though someone had rammed a metal rod up through her neck and shoulders. The long grasses scratched at her bare arms and face as they traveled. She was miserable but felt compelled to go on, even if they found her dead at the control.

As they skirted the edges of the rock strewn mountain passes, she strained her eyes for her first glimpse of Jappa's last forest. It was becoming dark rapidly, closing in around them like a thick, black glove, obliterating everything.

There were new mountains on the other side of the giants they edged, she noticed dully. A mist-filled valley ran down between the two massive formations then swirled over the black crags, creating gulfs and eddies in the spiring towers that ran on as far and wide as she could see.

When she realized what she faced, she abruptly hit the ski's foot control, falling to the ground hard. Her legs buckled beneath her, and she didn't have the strength to rise.

"What the hell are you doing?"

"The forest—it's the forest, isn't it?" she babbled. "It's so big."

He looked at her, shutting down his own ski. In the little light that remained, she was pale and drawn, sitting on the rocky ground, rubbing her arms. He realized that he had driven her like one of his own troops, which she wasn't. Doctor Fara Tucker was brilliant and dedicated and obviously stubborn, but she was also a research biologist and spent a large portion of her time in the lab.

"Let's stop until sunrise. It's too dark to travel safely." He couldn't quite bring himself to apologize; she hadn't protested, and they had made excellent time.

Arlington rummaged through his own sack in the eerie, green light that the striker created attached to one of the skis for power. There was a thermal sleeping bag and a large sealed pouch of some nameless food substance. He poured some of the food into a cup and handed it to her.

Wearily, she accepted it without a word and tasted it carefully. It was gelatinous and had very little smell or taste. It surged through her as she finished the cup and felt stronger.

"I remember this," she croaked then stopped, surprised to realize that what she heard was her own voice. "A friend of mine created it. We ate it for weeks to find out if it prevented dehydration."

"Next time, would you ask your friend to create something a little more appetizing?" He sat down on the ground opposite her and poured more of the gel into her cup.

"I really wasn't part of the project," she replied softly, swirling the food in her cup. "I'm basically—"

"A biological researcher with a heavy leaning toward making things reproduce."

"You could put it that way," she agreed. "I have done a lot of work with animals and plant infertility. That's how I developed the F 1. It wasn't really meant to work on plant life. It just seemed to work when we tried it on Miccah."

"What exactly do you think it will do?" He sipped his food.

"Well," she considered her words. "I believe there's every chance that the F 1 will cause the Singing Trees to start reproducing again. They did at one time, you know. Then suddenly something stopped them, caused them to go through a long spell of infertility. We're not really sure what that something was. The planet's history is too incomplete for that."

"In terms I can understand," he drawled, well acquainted with the tech jargon the Echo scientists used. "What does the F 1 do?"

"It works with a crystal whose resonance is a great deal like the trees themselves. It causes a vibration within the cells of the organism that changes their basic structure and alignment. They had to be fertile to begin with, you understand, for it to work. And we'll need to have the device placed at the sight of the last new growth, we estimate at about five hundred years ago."

Arlington tried to keep the sneer out of his voice. "What will that accomplish?"

"It should give the government something to think about, and with our help, they can start up new growth programs. Harvesting does go on successfully on many planets, Commander. In a few decades, they should be able to take what they need and replant with the new trees so that the supply never diminishes."

"The government of Jappa hasn't been notorious for conservation of anything."

"Then you and your Endo troops can come right in and force them to do what you want them to do," she spit out angrily, rubbing the scratches on her face. "But you will destroy this world when you do. This planet isn't just their wood or their government; it's their people as well. You saw them; you've studied them. How can you think soldiers patrolling the streets and overthrowing the government can make this world a better place?"

"At least the trees would be saved for the future," he retorted sharply.

"If that's all these people have are their Singing Trees, their lives will be over. No more music, no more dancing—but millions of trees guarded by soldiers."

"Doctor..." He drew in a deep breath. "Fara... we won't decide anything out here yelling at each other. I think this is why Central established two branches of the same unit—two methods, same objective. Always fighting over ideological fractions. Always competitive to get the job done."

Fara and her friends had discussed the same thing many

times. It was always the same—an honor they all dreaded to go into the field with their opposite. Echo always looked for the peaceful technological solution. Endo stomped and shouted their way in, demanding the environment be protected, strong arming anyone who dared to disagree.

"I have some salve for those scratches." He tossed a small vial to her. "It promises to grow new skin by morning. Maybe one of your babies?"

She smiled in the near darkness and caught the tube.

"No, but," she looked down and swallowed hard, her windblown hair curtaining her face, "you were right on Delta 7. There was no way to make those people understand that the water was poison and had to be cleaned." She looked up again and across at his lean, hard face. "But I do think—"

"Good night, Doctor. Morning comes early. Tomorrow's another day to argue."

Fara watched him slide down into the thermal sleeping bag before she joined him, timidly, turning her back to him as he did to her. "Good night, Commander. I appreciate your help."

"Such as it is," he answered gruffly, his voice muffled.

"I know it's the best you can do." She smiled and closed her eyes.

* * *

Something was wrong. There was no answer to his communication device the night before, but knowing that the trees' resonance interfered with communication, Matt had waited for the first sure light of morning. There was still no reply.

They shared the aero skis in the mist-shrouded morning. Conversation flared briefly then died. His group was gone. There were still remains of their last meal and a few stray pieces of clothing and equipment, but everyone had left.

Abruptly, from the look of it, he considered, hunched down to finger a track in the damp soil. Most importantly, the F 1 device was gone.

"Gone?" she questioned blankly. "Gone where?"

"I'm not sure. They must have taken it with them when they had to leave the check point. We'll have to find their location."

"There's not time." Fara rounded on him. "This wasn't part of some clever way to achieve your own goals, was it?"

"I thought we had all this worked out? We are basically on the same side. And while I might not agree with your methods, I wouldn't go against Central's decision any more than you would."

"Well there's no more time to waste," she told him calmly. "You never had the device. I couldn't trust anyone to transport it here safely. So I brought it myself."

He looked at the battered brown case on the ground at her feet. "The device was in the case that you nearly lost at the port? Was that safe transportation?"

"At least I know where it is, and I have it with me now. I didn't lose it." She glared at him "And a group of troops."

They stood in the clearing mist and stared at each other, anger flaring between them.

"We have to get moving." Fara turned away quickly, grabbing her case and her ski. "We're not that far from the rendezvous point with my contact."

Arlington followed her lead. "We're probably about an hour from the south marker on the map."

She nodded, pushing in the pedal on her ski. Fara ignored him and kept her mind on where they were going. She hung on grimly to the specter of her failure on Delta 7, determined nothing like it would happen on Jappa. She had nearly forgotten how important the contract for Jappa was to Echo. Apparently, Commander Arlington hadn't.

The terrain was easier to negotiate once they left the mountains heading south through the forest. The heavy tree growth kept the forest floor clear of grass or large foliage. The aero skis hummed in the silence, swiftly flashing through the early morning mist.

Fara brushed aside Arlington's attempt to give her another nutri wafer, concentrat¬ing her attention on the map of Jappa's primal forest she'd tapped up on her wrist monitor.

According to her calculations, they were approaching the southeast quadrant. They rapidly approached a small shrine her contact had mentioned. She powered down the ski, this time gliding slowly to the ground as she'd seen the Commander do earlier.

She waited for him impatiently. "We'll have to go on foot from here. We're about two kilometers from the holy shrine of Jappa's Singing Trees. My contact is there, but we'll have to approach as pilgrims. All other contact is strictly forbidden."

Arlington, putting aside his own anger, glanced suggestively at his own bright red uniform with obvious Endo insignia then at her Echo blues.

"I thought about that problem, Commander, although I didn't think about you being here." She put her case down and opened it, pulling out a shrink garment that expanded in the air to a gray coverall with a heavy hood. It was sizes too large for her but covered her uniform completely. "I guess you'll have to stay here until I finish."

"Fortunately for you," he replied coolly, "I have a rain cover that will have to do as my pilgrim gear. But I'd go with you if it was in full dress uniform."

They hid the aero skis in some tall grass and argued briefly over her obviously offworld case. Fara finally agreed to put the F 1 device in his cloth carry sack but insisted that she would carry it herself.

She chewed the nutri wafer that Arlington had finally nagged her into eating as they walked through the gray-brown shadows of the damp forest. It was as though she could feel the age of the trees and the land around them, even though she could not feel the resonance.

"What does it feel like?" she wondered, breaking their

long silence.

The powerful urge of the trees was such that it could not be ignored, and he didn't pretend not to know what she was talking about. "I have a friend whose library is built of wood from Jappa. It's hard to define the feeling. Euphoria, well-being, like taking a deep breath and knowing that everything will work out all right."

"But the sound," she insisted.

"Like music but less defined, sweeter but with no tune. It's like good wine tingling through your body. It fills empty places that you didn't know were empty."

"No wonder everyone here dances in the streets and loses themselves in the song."

"And why they aren't able to manage their own problems," he reminded her. "I've often wondered if all the government workers have to wear impeding devices. I do know that they use the resonance as a punishment. They take it away from prisoners and logging workers unless they cooperate."

The shrine came into view down a long, damp stretch of ground that had been trampled by countless feet before theirs. There were few pilgrims near the tiny wooden frame hut that morning. Some were asleep on the ground outside. Others were in heated debate near the doorway that was a simple, open arch.

"Any of them look familiar?" Arlington asked her quietly as they approached the hut.

"I've never met him," she conceded. "We have an understanding. We'll have to give each pilgrim the holy salute." She thought she heard him groan.

She proceeded to greet all of the pilgrims at the shrine except for the sleeping ones. Arlington stood to one side, watching the group.

One of the sleeping pilgrims was covered by brush, snoring loudly near the doorway. Fara approached him carefully, wrinkling her nose as she neared him. What her race couldn't hear, they made up for in olfactory. The pilgrim hadn't bathed or changed his dirty robe in a long time. She hoped it would not be him that she was supposed to meet.

Of course it was.

"You're late," he told her after snorting and wheezing into alertness. He cleared his sinuses on a nearby brush.

"I had some problems getting here," she explained, revolted but committed.

He followed her gaze to where the commander stood against a tree. "You'll have to tell him not to touch the Trees. They are sacred. Holy. We never touch Them."

She nodded. "I'll tell him. Are you ready to go?"

He rubbed his dirty face with an equally dirty hand. "Do you have anything to eat?"

"Of course. I'll just—"

He lifted his robe and relieved himself on the ground.

Fara looked away, catching Arlington's quiet laughter. "Don't touch the trees," she said, approaching him. "They're holy."

"Is this your paragon of knowledge?"

"Yes. He's ready to go, but he needs some food."

"Is that all?"

"As far as I know."

"He's helping you because the trees are holy?" Arlington watched the pilgrim put down his robe and waddle toward them.

"Some people are like that," she protested his covert suggestions.

"How did he contact you?"

"Not now," she hissed as the pilgrim came closer. "Martok," she introduced them, "this is Commander Arlington."

Martok nodded solemnly. "Where's the food?"

"I'll get it," Fara obliged.

"Let's get started then. It's a long way."

The forest became cooler and greener as they went

deeper into the leaf strewn interior. Red moss hung low from boughs that were thicker than a human body. Tiny strips of sunlight dappled the ground between the heavy leaves that soared at least one hundred meters against the sky.

Arlington worked with his communicator, trying to locate his missing group of troops as they walked closer to the prime area of new growth. There was no response. No way of knowing if it was the trees or his group was unable to answer.

"He doesn't trust me." Martok smiled, looking up to where the sky would be.

Fara glanced behind them at the commander. "He doesn't trust anyone. It's his job."

"Is it your job as well?"

"No. We work for the same people, but we're totally different. His answers are not my answers."

"No. I can see that. Tell me again what the device will do for the Holy Ones."

"It will help them to be able to reproduce again, to have young ones as it was before."

"That was so long ago. None of us can know what that was like. Or that it is what they want. " He studied her face. "Can we be sure it is what we want?"

Fara considered his words. She had tested and retested the F 1 device. It had to work. Martok didn't realize the implications for his people if it didn't.

Arlington gave up on his communicator and walked closer to the pair in front of him. They were discussing the mythos of the planet and the trees in particular.

"They say," Martok sang in his sage's warble, "when the prime forest was new, that the Holy Ones began to sing. When they sang, the air was glad and the beasts also. But no fruit shall they bear while the song continues, until time past."

"What does that mean?" Arlington asked when the

pilgrim stopped the chant.

"No one knows. It comes down from the Holy Ones to us. We accept on faith." Martok smiled at them both and belched. Then he stopped dead. "I can go no further."

"Great." Arlington pushed his hood back from his head.

"What's wrong?" Fara asked. "You said you'd take me to the prime area."

"We approach it. In the next glade. But I cannot enter. No one who knows the ways of the Holy Ones may enter. The song is too strong. It would destroy our minds," Martok explained, sitting down on the ground. "I'll wait here for your return."

Arlington took his weapon out and handed another to Fara. "I'll bet he will. There's probably more than just strong singing down there."

She hefted the carry sack closer to her side. "We have to go in."

"Walk to the center where it is deepest," Martok counselled as they started forward. "You will know the place."

"Do you feel any different?" Fara wondered as they disappeared into the darkness.

"Yes," he answered coldly. "I feel like a fool for walking into this. No back up, just a research biologist with a reproductive device and a tree priest waiting to finish off our provisions."

"I meant the resonance. Are you still shielded?"

"Apparently. I don't feel like dancing yet. Stay close."

"How will we know the place?" she asked aloud, seeing nothing but blackness around them.

"There's some sort of clearing ahead," Arlington told her, walking in front. "Stay here. Let me check it out before you bring the device in. Will you?"

"All right." She took out the weapon he'd given her. "I can use this if I need to."

"Good. Stay here but stay ready."

He walked slowly down into the clearing, the sunlight from the dancing leaves glittering on the wet bark of the last trees. There were three trees standing together, making a close ring in the denseness. The ground around their mammoth, protruding roots was soggy with runoff water. The scent of dirt was suffocating.

There was no denying a new, buzzing sound through his head. It wasn't overwhelm¬ing as Martok had insisted, but that was only due to the deflector in his ear. It brought with it a tingling awareness that seeped into his limbs, making him feel as though he were sinking into the wet ground.

"Is everything all right?" Fara called from outside the ring of trees.

"Yes," he answered, but even to his own ears the sound was slurred.

She inched her way into the heart of the forest with careful footsteps, occasionally dragging her foot out of the sticky leaf rot and dirt, clinging to her carry bag. When her eyes adjusted to the darkness, she could see Arlington sitting on one of the roots.

"This is it," she said, climbing into the circle near him. "The last of the trees to grow. The baby of all the Holy Ones on Jappa."

"What now?"

"We set up the device and hope it works," she decided. "Are you all right?"

"I will be," he answered slowly. "I think it's the resonance, like the old man said."

"Good thing you have the deflector." She took the F 1 out of the bag. The prototype was small, much smaller than the original device she'd created. A new power source had allowed for the shift in size and weight.

She swallowed hard and looked at the trees surrounding her. They were easily five hundred years old. Nowhere that they had walked in the forest had she seen a single sign of new growth. She couldn't hurt the trees if the device killed them. The loggers were coming tomorrow.

The F 1 device was in place in the circle of youngest trees. She looked up at Arlington, surprised to find his gaze already on her.

"Power up," he said encouragingly.

Fara nodded. With an indrawn breath and a slightly shaking hand, she started the power accelerator.

Arlington felt the change at once. The resonance from the closest trees became stronger, more piercing. He put his hands to his ears, the sound too powerful for the deflector's range.

Someone screamed from outside the dark glen. It had to be Martok.

She urged the commander to his feet, but he seemed unable to move, his face screwed up tightly in pain. She looked up at the trees, the sunlight, and nothing seemed different to her. The F 1 device hummed quietly, the changing pulses racing through the tree's roots.

There was shouting from outside the darkness. A split shaft of a power blaster ricocheted off the tree nearest the device. More shots followed and the muffled sounds of running feet.

"We have to move." Fara grabbed wildly at Arlington's arm. "We have to get away from the device."

He shook his head, trying to rise, reaching for his weapon. His brain was blistered with the shrieking of the resonance. Only duty and years of discipline brought him up. He fired his blaster into the forest from the direction of the first shot.

"They'll follow us if we leave," she tried to explain. "We have to lead them away from the device."

Stumbling, Fara half dragging him through the mud and debris as the government troops continued to fire at them, they left the circle of trees behind in the close blackness.

Martok was prostrate on the ground, babbling formless chants to the trees. She called to him, but he couldn't answer.

"Grab his arm," Arlington shouted, doing the same on the man's other side.

"Are you all right?" she asked breathlessly.

"There was something there in that circle." He shook his head. "I can't explain. But it's gone now. I can still feel the resonance, but it's not as strong."

With Martok between them, they groped their way through the dim recess of the forest. There were screams from the blackness where the government troops followed through the ring of trees. Commander Arlington returned fire from one or two more shots. Then the forest was silent as though it had swallowed up the men behind them.

Martok was dead weight, and the ground was wet and slippery, making their progress slow. When they reached a clearing, Arlington called to Fara to stop, and they waited. There were no sounds of pursuit.

"Where are they?" She almost wished she could see the troops rather than feeling the eerie quiet.

"Maybe the same thing that hit me over there got them. My deflector should have tuned out all the resonance, but I could feel it before you started the device. And after..."

"Was that your doing?" Martok asked at length, tears running down his face.

Fara shrugged and looked across at Arlington.

"Something in the resonance changed. It was like screaming," he responded. "It was like the damn trees were screaming."

"It has been so long." Martok's eyes were glazed as he looked up at the trees. "They had forgotten the feeling of being alive. They have slept for so long. Now they've awakened."

She didn't believe the trees could scream, but his words made her shiver. There was no way to know until she could do some testing whether the F 1 had done its job. Martok and Arlington's strange reaction was out of the ordinary, but that didn't classify as proof.

"Of course." Martok laughed and cried at once. "It is painful for Them, as it would be for you or me, to use a part of ourselves that had been asleep for so long. They groan, and They sigh. But it is good. It is very good."

"When will you know what's happened?" Arlington asked slowly, looking away from the jubilant holy man. "How much of the forest will it affect?"

"In theory, only ten percent," she whispered. "We'll have to wait—"

"All. All are alive and awake," Martok declared. "The sign will come. You will see."

"We need to get out of here. It will be only a matter of time before they throw off the effect and come after us. We need to find—" He looked down at his communicator. In amazement, he touched the crystal and heard a clear voice break through on the open channel.

"Something's happened, Commander," his second-in-command stated brokenly. "The communicator is on line. Give us your position for pick up."

Arlington saw troops crawling out of the forest into the clearing before he saw their shattered faces. He cautiously removed the resonance deflectors from his own ears. There was nothing.

Fara sat cross-legged on the ground, using her computer to calculate the effect of the vibrations from the device. Even if the power source had been stronger, she couldn't hope to reach all the trees. If just a few would be fertile...

"It's gone." Matt knelt down beside her. "The resonance is gone."

"You're letting the situation cloud your judgement, Commander," she assured him. "The vibrations can only reach—"

"All." Martok was certain. "They are joined." He linked

his fingers together to show his meaning. "They have always been this way."

"Their roots are joined," she theorized slowly. "That could account for a larger percentage but not all."

"Look at them," Arlington advised her, glancing at the troops, their uniforms filthy with mud, their eyes wide with shock. "The music is gone. The Singing Trees are silent."

Fara strained with all her being to hear or not hear some snatch of resonance, but there was nothing for her—as there had been nothing there since she arrived. "Are you sure?"

"Look at them. And you know I don't make judgements without facts. The device must have changed the resonance of the trees, just as Central thought, only the resonance didn't change. It stopped."

"The Holy Ones have reached the time of awakenings." Martok smiled beatifically at them both. "It would have come even without your device, as it was foretold."

"The device accelerated the process," she considered, trying to rationalize what had happened. "But all the trees…"

"I don't know." Arlington tried to help her but was left floundering for the answer. "It will damn sure solve the problem of harvesting. No music in the wood to cut and sell."

"But the people," she protested. "This will be more devastating than if your commandos had come in and taken over. No more music."

"Central will send in social aiders. They'll help them through it." He shrugged, suddenly feeling good. "As I said before, a dose of reality won't hurt these people. Maybe they'll even come to appreciate what they have here."

"I can't even be sure the process worked, that the trees are able to reproduce now. It could all be in vain." She looked at him from anguished eyes. What had she done?

Matt tapped in the coordinates and sent the message on to his group. "They should be here in a few minutes. Central will want a full report on this as quickly as possible."

Fara got up from her wet seat on the ground and looked

into the faces of the amazed and silent group of soldiers. How would they adjust? She wanted to save the music so badly for them all. Now they might never hear it again. Their world would be as empty and silent as her own.

In trying to prevent her fate from happening to Jappa, she had brought it to them.

"Do not mourn." Martok approached her. "Just as was foretold, the Holy Ones will bear fruit now that the song is silent. But They will sing again when the time for sleep has come and the forests are full and green."

"How can you be so sure?" She wiped a tear from her dirty face.

"The sign has been promised us," he told her confidently.

She wished she could believe in signs and omens as he did, but there was no proof that could guarantee that the trees would sing again. The sun was setting scarlet and gold behind the huge, old trees. They reached towards the darkening sky where a sprinkling of stars danced in their leafy boughs.

Fara heard the soft whirr of Endo's vehicles approaching in the twilight. She sighed and brushed her hand along a low-lying bough. A fragrance twitched at her senses, and there was a damp velvet under her fingers.

"Behold," Martok whispered. "The miracle of life begins."

She stroked the pale pink of the small, delicate bloom on the long black branch and thought that perhaps there was music in the night after all.

The Magician and the Sorceress-Accountant

The magic of love can blur the boundaries of space and time. Just ask Skye Mertz as she drives the Taxi For The Dead. For your reading pleasure, here is a tale of a modern-day sorceress who finds her one true wish is not what she desired. It takes a powerful mage, conjured from time-knows-when—not unlike Lucas—to show her where her power truly lies.

"With power and light I call thee. With chalk and powder I capture thee. With my will do I bend thee to my bidding. Come forth to me!"

Nothing happened. She opened her eyes and looked around the room, but it was the same. The lines of power glowed around the pentagram, but it was still empty inside the marking.

Slightly daunted, she closed her eyes and repeated the incantation. Again, nothing happened.

Lacie had taken three days off to be sure that her concentration wasn't pulled away from her project. She'd cleaned her apartment thoroughly, paying particular attention to that spot in her living room where the carpet was pulled back. With a steady hand, she'd drawn the pentagram on the floor in pencil then repeated the image with the special chalk that glowed in the dark. In the center of it, she'd placed a comfortable chair and a small table with a candle and a basket of fruit.

Blessing herself, she'd slipped out of her clothes and grimaced at herself in the mirror. It had been a reminder of why this was so important.

Not that she needed one. She'd always been a fat girl. First a fat baby, then a fat child, and then a fat woman. Nothing she did seemed to make any difference. There were actresses and models that were the fashionable size zero, while she could barely maintain a size sixteen!

The time had come for action.

Clearing her mind of the past and her feelings of inferiority, she held the magical powder in her hand. She closed her eyes and spoke the words of power. The pentagram glowed, illuminating the room, and then dimmed.

She rechecked the lines and added what was left of the powder to them. She rechecked her incantation. She was saying the words right. Why wasn't it working? She looked at the table and the chair.

Bingo! She'd forgotten the most important part of the spell. She needed the personal item that would draw the person to her. Careful not to put any part of her into the pentagram, Lacie tossed the scrap of ancient text inside the lines.

Going back around the lines, she closed her eyes and focused. "With power and light I call thee. With chalk and powder I capture thee. With my will do I bend thee to my bidding. Come forth to me!"

Lacie felt a tremendous surge of power along the lines she'd drawn. The room was bright as day. A strong breeze ruffled her hair and blew the curtains. The energy pulsated in blue lines around the markings. Careful to stand away from the light, she was still touched by the raw power of the spell. It was like being hit between the eyes with a cement block.

Dazed, she sat on the floor and ruefully rubbed her aching head. All of her implements for the spell lay around her. She was naked, and her bright red hair was in wild disarray on her shoulders. She looked around the room, but nothing had changed. She'd failed again.

"Woman!" someone bellowed at her. "What dost thou?"

She blinked and looked through the slowly fading light. Something had changed.

There was a man inside her pentagram!

She got to her feet. Was it the right man?

"What dost thou, sorceress?"

"Please stop shouting," Lacie requested, putting a hand to her head. "You'll wake my neighbors, and my head hurts."

"As well it might," he concluded. "What were thou thinking to bring me here? What manner of creature are thee?"

"I'm a human just like you," she told him, picking up the aspirin bottle and shoving four of them into her mouth, sloshing water down after them. "I'm not a sorceress."

"I am captured in a mystical pentagram." He stuck his finger to the invisible wall above the lines and energy flared back at him. "If thou art not a sorceress, what manner of demon art thou?"

"I'm not a demon either." She looked at him, awestruck by what she'd done. "Cagliastro? Count Cagliastro?"

"You know my name?"

"I read all about you—Cagliastro, magician to the kings of France and Italy, necromancer, master of time and space. Most think you were born around 1200 AD, but there are no records for your death. Your life was shadowed, filled with secrecy. You tried to change base metals into gold."

"How come you to know so much about me, sorceress?"

"I'm not really a sorceress! I'm just... well, desperate, I guess."

"And powerful!" He folded his arms across his chest. "Just what may be so important that you summon me when I am on the threshold of my greatest achievement?"

"You mean changing base metals into gold?" She sat in the chair she'd set out for herself outside the pentagram.

"Please! No one ever did that, and no one ever will. Gold is gold. I know you guys all thought it was possible, but it's just not."

"You guys?" Cagliastro's mouth formed around the words then spit them out at her. "What are you guys?"

Lacie looked at the richness of his gold and purple robe. The light glinted on the strands of real gold spun into the material. He was much bigger than she'd expected. His powerful arms and chest suggested that he either worked out or had a spell for maintaining muscle.

"You guys are the group of sorcerers and conjurers who tried to change lead and other base metals into gold. It never worked for any of you. Not even close."

"What sayest thou, sorceress?"

"I'm not a sorceress," she repeated and glanced around the room. "Okay, it looks like I'm a sorceress, but I'm just an accountant with a good credit card. I bought all of this stuff then used it to bring you here."

"Accountant?"

"Someone who does people's taxes."

"Ah, taxes! These I understand." He smiled shrewdly. "Thou needs gold to pay these taxes? Is that why thou hast brought me here?"

"No, I don't pay the taxes. I figure them out for other people." She ran a hand over her hair. "But that's not why I brought you here."

"But thou dost admit thine sorcery brought me here to you?"

"Yes, I admit that, I guess. But I'll let you go again if you'll tell me the secret for transferring mass."

Cagliastro's eyes were a strange shade of blue/black. "Thou dost have need of me then."

"Yes," she admitted with a shiver, feeling those eyes in the recesses of her soul. "But not for making gold or anything like that. I read once that you could transfer mass from one thing to another. I have some mass I want to transfer to something else."

"What mass is this, woman?"

"Well," she began, the words catching like dough in her throat, "most of the...mass on me. I have a special pot to transfer it to."

He put back his head and roared with laughter. His strange eyes pinned her in place. "Thou hast brought me here to make thou skinny and unappealing to men? If I were not greatly amused by this ridiculous use of my power and knowledge, I would strike thou dead!"

Lacie winced. "Okay, first of all, I don't think you can do that."

"Dost thou challenge me to learn?"

She glanced along the lines of the powerful pentagram she'd created. "I guess so."

"So be it, witch!" He raised his hand, and a blinding flash of green light shot out from his finger. It touched the glowing blue edge of the pentagram and bounced back. He walked around the pentagram attacking it in various places, but he couldn't breach her creation.

"I was pretty careful," she told him.

"So I see," he replied, stopping his attack. "And if I refuse to grant thy request?"

"Well, then I guess you'll be stuck here and all of that making gold out of lead will be left to the other guys."

Cagliastro roared his anger at her and stabbed the blue pentagram until it sizzled with energy, but he couldn't breach it. "I shall not be made to help thee, sorceress-accoun-tant!"

She stood up. "Well, then I guess you'll be here for a while. There's a comfortable chair. There's fruit. I can throw you a magazine if you like."

"I shall not be your prisoner, woman! My wrath will be the death of you!"

Lacie gulped. She could feel the waves of power coming from him, even though the pentagram held him in check.

"M-maybe I should turn on the television for you." She

switched on the set behind her. "I have to go and lie down now. My head is killing me."

"When I escape from this prison, your head will be severed from your body and eaten by jackals!"

"O-okay. Well, think about the mass transfer. I'll let you go as soon as you agree to do it."

"Argghh!" Flashes of blue mingled with flashes of green power.

"G-good night."

He roared in the other room. She closed her bedroom door and somehow managed to fall asleep as soon as her head hit the pillow. She didn't dream and was grateful for it. Cagliastro had been pretty graphic in his threats.

Lacie was awakened by a combination of the doorbell and the telephone. The apartment was smoky with the remnants of energy and candles that had gone out hours before. She looked at the clock and realized she'd slept straight through to the next day. The living room was quiet.

Had Cagliastro escaped?

She answered the phone first, a little disoriented.

"Lacie, where are you? You should have been here at eight for the meeting."

"I know," she agreed, "I'm sorry, Jimmy. I've been sick." She coughed a few times.

"You were off on vacation the last three days!"

"I know. But now I'm sick. I need a sick day."

He sighed dramatically. "Fine. Just get back in here tomorrow."

"Thanks, Jimmy."

"Don't thank me. Thank the fact that you're a damned good accountant!"

Lacie put down the phone and walked carefully out of her room. The doorbell was still buzzing. She didn't have the nerve to glance into the living room.

It was Jennifer Arnold from the apartment next door. "What the hell is going on in here?"

"What? Uh…nothing. Nothing. I've been sick."

"Well, you're damned noisy about it! Was that you doing all the shouting? It sounded like a man!" Her neighbor's perfect red lips curled into a smile. "Do you have a man in here, sweetie?"

"Well, uh—"

"Did he come home with you from Overeater's Anonymous?"

Lacie wished she had Jennifer trapped in the pentagram. "I have to go now."

"Wait." She pushed at the door. "Don't I get to meet him? I'm your neighbor!"

"Go away, Jennifer."

Jennifer smirked at Lacie's pink robe. "If he loves you in that thing, he must love you."

Lacie closed the door and locked it with both locks. She made a face at Jennifer through it then crept carefully into the living room.

Despite his threats to harm her, Lacie felt sure Cagliastro had escaped during the night and simply went back to his own time. To her surprise, he was still inside the pentagram.

To her further surprise, he'd brought other things to him. The pentagram had stretched to encompass a huge, ornate bed made of gold inlaid wood. The sheets were stark white, and the blanket was sewn with golden thread. There was a table and a desk, both covered in scrolls and bound texts. Cagliastro was watching the morning traffic report on television, and he looked up as she walked into the room.

She stared at him, suddenly aware of the enormity of what she'd done. The magician sat in the air, floating about three feet above the floor where a gorgeous carpet was now spread to all the lines of the pentagram. A lighted, gold lamp hovered in the air above him. What now?

"Did I awaken thine neighbor, sorceress?" His tones were softer.

Lacie smiled, relieved. "She heard you yelling, but—"

"Good!" he yelled again. "I would waken every man, woman, and child in this cursed time until you free me!"

"Just do what I asked you to do," she replied, shuddering despite herself. What had she done, and how could she get out of it? "I'll let you go."

He peered at her slyly. "I have observed thy world on this screen. Why dost thou want to be unappealing to men? Art thou femme butch?"

She smiled. "You must be watching too much television."

"Release me from this prison."

"Not until we have a deal."

"What is this deal?" Cagliastro narrowed his eyes.

"A pact. You know. I give you something you want, and you give me the mass transfer."

"How do you know this?"

"I read it in a book." Lacie looked at his darkly handsome face. He was a very attractive man. That she found him attractive brought her back to her original purpose. If she backed away now, she would never do it again. She was caught in a trap of her own making. But so was he.

"Well, I don't have to work again today, so maybe we can come to some mutually beneficial agreement," she attempted to communicate with him.

"Thou works? Thou are enslaved?" He studied her, walking within the pentagram like a caged tiger.

She shivered. She knew who lunch would be if he got out. "No, we don't have slaves anymore. I mean, there was a war, and people just don't do that kind of thing. Well, at least not in this country. I work to make a living. People pay me to do their taxes and create special accounts where they can hide their assets."

"How much do these people pay thou?"

"Enough. I've been there a while, and I do pretty well. Jimmy knows I could take half the clients if I left."

"Jimmy?"

"My boss."

Cagliastro considered the word. "Your lover?"

Lacie laughed bitterly. "Hardly."

"But you desire him?"

"He only dates really thin women, like a size zero."

"How can one be less than a number?" He drew his brows together.

"It happens," she answered. "That's all I want from you. Mass transfer. From me to this."

He looked at her and at the big black pot she held. "Of all the skills I have mastered, this is the one you crave?"

"I just want to be thin," she replied in an anguished tone. "I've tried everything. Diets, exercise, but this is the best I can do."

Cagliastro's eyes followed the lines of her body. "Thou art lush and womanly. Why would a man want a twig in his arms?"

Lacie blushed beet red to her scalp.

He nodded, finally understanding. "Thou art old to be a virgin."

"I'm not that old."

"How old art thou?"

"Twenty-six." She bit her lip.

"I can well understand thy desperation!"

"I don't care about Jimmy," she told him. "My sister is getting married in two weeks. She's gorgeous and thin. I want to be thin for her wedding. That's all."

"Thou lies to thineself, but not to Cagliastro! I can see thine heart, sorceress-accountant."

She resisted the urge to stomp her foot in frustration. "Don't call me that!"

"What else shall I call thee? Thou hast given me no name."

"I'm Lacie D—" She stopped, realizing that he'd almost tricked her into making a mistake. If he knew her real name, her whole name, he could use it against her. Blue-black eyes warred with green, but Lacie pulled away from his considerable power.

"Lacie D," he said when he realized she would give up nothing more. His voice had turned seductive, sliding through her senses like a sheet of silk. "Thy name suits thou."

"All you have to do is help me." She moved away from the edge of the pentagram.

"And what will I receive in return, Lacie D?"

She grimaced at the name but didn't correct him again. They'd reached the stage that the spell book had said, where they bargained for his release. It seemed like progress, anyway.

Opening a small, velvet pouch, she offered him an old brooch that had belonged to her grandmother. "It's pure gold. The diamond in the center is real."

The brooch was worth a fortune. It was the only thing she had from her maternal grandmother, but the book said it had to be valuable in both worth and sentiment.

Cagliastro's eyes lit up when he saw the brooch. He reached out his hand for it, but the pentagram's power lay between them. He pulled back sharply. "Not for ten times that would I help thee!"

Lacie put the brooch back in the pouch. "I guess you can make yourself at home then."

"Get thee from my sight, Lacie D, sorceress-accountant!" He looked away from her. "I can bide my time here until your time is gone."

She never guessed he'd be so stubborn or so crafty! She could see the clever intelligence in his beautiful eyes. He'd trick her if he could. She was going to have to be careful. Who would've thought he'd be so averse to helping her, even with the promise of the brooch?

And who'd have guessed he'd be so attractive? She took a deep breath. She'd been expecting someone older. Or maybe he was old, and it was an illusion? She was way in over her head. She needed help.

Lacie got dressed and spent about an hour studying her books. People captured in the pentagram were supposed to be cooperative. They wanted to be released. Why had she picked someone who didn't care? How could she bargain with him for release and her safety if he didn't want anything she had to offer?

Cagliastro lounged back in his chair, one black-panted leg thrown carelessly across an elaborately carved wooden arm. A purple and gold shirt covered his black under-tunic. The shirt showed off the width of his shoulders and the darkness of his hair. He smiled at Lacie and saluted her with his teacup when she returned. He was watching the President's jet take off on CNN.

She sat down hard on the chair outside the pentagram. "If I let you go, will you swear that you won't hurt me or anyone else because of this?"

He put down his cup. "Are you releasing me?"

"I don't know. I didn't expect it to be this hard."

"I have actually enjoyed my time here. I shall make you a pact, Lacie D."

Her eyebrows went up. "You will?"

"You will release me and teach me about your time. In turn, I will transfer the mass from you as you requested."

"Really? Why?"

"I could go out into your world, but I would be as a sheep lost amidst the brambles in a storm. Your television has been interesting, but I hunger to see the world as it is now. It is a new millennium, full of wonders. Wouldst thou show it to me, Lacie D?"

She thought for a moment. "How can I trust you?"

"Do your books not tell you that a pact made within the pentagram is a pact that must be honored?"

That was true. It was the only way to bargain with someone trapped in the drawing. "So you're giving me your word that you will transfer the mass to the pot in exchange for me releasing you and showing you the twenty-first century? And that you won't hurt anyone?"

"That is the pact," he agreed, putting out his hand. "Do you agree?"

Lacie considered it. It seemed almost too easy, but she was desperate in more ways than one. If she touched him or put her hand through the line of power, she would be vulnerable. It would be too late to take it back. But she couldn't keep him trapped there forever.

She had no choice but to go forward with her plan.

Carefully, she slid her shaking hand into his. His fingers closed around it, warm and firm, and the power lines began to fade. Lacie closed her eyes. If he was going to kill her, she didn't want to know. It wasn't like she could stop him once she'd touched him.

"Open your eyes, Lacie D." Cagliastro stood in front of her, still holding her hand. He was dark and distinctly handsome, but he was wearing jeans and a black t-shirt that emphasized his chest and arms. His blue-black eyes held her gaze. "Did you doubt my word?"

"Maybe. A little."

He pulled her to her feet. "Come. I hunger for a vision of this new world."

"Mass transfer," she reminded him weakly.

"Later. I have been confined in this place for too long. You already have my word."

The raw energy running from his hand through her made her shiver. It wasn't magic, at least not the kind from the book. Cagliastro wasn't just a magician from the past. He was a handsome hunk of a magician in modern gear. Lacie couldn't take her eyes off of him.

"Where do you want to start?"

"I have seen many things on your television. Take me to them."

"Well, suppose we go out and start there. We can decide as we go."

"I know you will honor your part of the pact."

Lacie drew in a deep breath and led him from the apartment.

Cagliastro was amazed by everything. Electricity and flushing toilets, tacos and music from CDs, all made him smile and ask for more. He was like a child in a candy store. In fact, she took him to a candy store and a toy store. They walked through a computer store, and she explained technology. Lacie didn't own a car, but she took him to a dealership where they let him drive one. She showed him the basics, and he took off down the street.

"I am amazed! How is all of this possible?" he said when they'd returned.

"I don't know. It's been a long time coming from 1200 AD. We've had a lot of time to work on things."

"I never dreamed this could be!" He marveled at the tall buildings around him. "My own abilities seem small compared to these things."

"I think they're just different. I wouldn't call floating in the air nothing."

"That amazed you?"

She smiled. "I was pretty amazed."

"I shall teach you the trick before I leave you."

"Thanks."

He grinned at her mischievously. "And you will teach me a trick in return."

"Okay." She went quickly through her list of tricks. "How about this?"

Lacie took a quarter, turned it over in her hand, and then opened her palm.

"Where?" He looked into her hand.

She reached behind his ear and pulled out the quarter. "My Uncle Bob taught me that."

Cagliastro laughed, taking her arm in his hand. "I knew you were a sorceress, Lacie D."

"I wish!" She scuffed her foot on the pavement.

"There is only one magical quality you lack to be a sorceress." He touched her chin, lifting her face to his.

She felt breathless being so close to him. "What is that?"

"You must learn to love yourself."

"I will," she pledged, her face tingling where he'd touched her. "A soon as we do the mass transfer."

He frowned but did not reply.

They spent the entire day together and well into the night. When the city lights came on, Cagliastro caught his breath. They rode the subway until Lacie fell asleep on his shoulder.

When they got back to her apartment, Lacie went for the black pot that would hold the excess mass of her body. Cagliastro closed the door behind them and watched her eagerly await that moment when she would be perfect.

"First there is something I must show you."

"You gave me your word," she reminded him.

"And I do not break it. But first there is something you must see. You have a looking glass?"

"Yes."

"Must I guess where you hide it?"

"No. It's this way." She took a deep breath and led him to her enemy, the full- length mirror on the back of her bedroom door.

Before she could move, he took her arm and held her in front of the mirror. He stood behind her. His eyes were fierce on hers in the reflection.

"I have learned today that you have a warm, loving heart, Lacie D," he told her in a deep voice. "You have compassion and beauty. But you care nothing for those."

"I—"

"Quiet, woman! You have asked me here. I will speak."

Lacie stared at him until she felt his hands come around her. They caressed her body in the mirror. She groaned and closed her eyes.

"No, you will see this," he commanded. "Open your

eyes. Watch me love you."

She would've protested. She would've told him to stop.

But there in the mirror, she was beautiful.

He undressed her slowly, exquisitely. He told her what he was going to do, exciting her, and then his mouth claimed hers. His hand caressed her breasts until she wasn't sure her legs would hold her upright. He made love to her in the mirror with his whispered words and his strong hands.

Lacie moaned when his lips touched her throat. She forgot to look at herself or at him, swept away by the powerful emotions that thrilled through her. She wanted him as she had never wanted another man in her life. She didn't know if it was something he'd done to her or just chemistry that couldn't be explained. But by the time he came to her, she was ready for him, inviting him to her with her hands and her mouth.

Through the long night, he was there beside her, loving her, touching her, never letting her go.

But in the morning, she was alone. Chilled by the cool air, she huddled under the blankets and realized that he wasn't there anymore. He'd gone back to his own time. She could feel his absence in her heart.

But he'd kept his word. Better than his word. Her hair was fuller, less penny-bright or frizzy. Her skin was smoother and had an aura of luster to it. Her eyes were greener.

And her body was thin! She danced around the room naked. She was as thin as a model!

When she went out, men stared at her. They ran to get doors for her and asked her out for dates. Jimmy gave up his girlfriend in the hope that Lacie might date him. She bought a huge new wardrobe that was tight and fit her in all the right places.

And she had never been unhappier.

Lacie stared at the pentagram lines that had been under her rug and thought about Cagliastro. She'd turned down a date that night to sit by herself. Men wanted her now, and it was a powerful knowledge.

What she hadn't considered was that she wouldn't want them. She wanted the dark magician. She wanted him to come to her in the night and touch her. She wasn't a fat, twenty-six-year-old virgin anymore. She was a woman in love with a man she couldn't have, no matter how thin she had become.

It was probably just some leftover magic, but she missed him.

Despite phone calls, flowers, and messages on her computer, Lacie ignored most of the other men for the rest of the time until her sister's wedding. She didn't have a date and didn't want one. Her family was going to be shocked at her appearance.

Even that didn't matter anymore.

Her sister could have the rich Texan. She only wanted Cagliastro.

Lonelier than she'd ever been in her life, she slipped into her poofy, violet bridesmaids' dress. Her father was coming for her in half an hour. She brushed her hair and looked at herself. Even the terrible dress couldn't take away from her glowing new beauty and thin body.

The doorbell rang. She was ready to go, even though her heart wasn't in it.

She opened her mouth to speak, but no words came out. It was Cagliastro. He wore a dark suit with a purple tie and gleaming white shirt and held an exotic white flower in his hand.

"For you."

Lacie took the flower. The perfume made her head swim. "Why are you— Where did you come from?"

"Once you introduced me to your time, I could come and go as I pleased. I needed only a landmark to bring me back. Not that I needed any building or street. I have you."

"Oh. Why?"

"Why did I come back?" He smiled, and her knees felt weak. She just nodded, not trusting herself to speak. "Because I find that I have been lonely. I crave you, Lacie. If you are brave enough to come with me."

"I—"

"You are happy with you new form? Men adore you?"

"Yes... no. Men have been nice to me. But I—"

He looked around. "You are going to your sister's wedding with no escort?"

She nodded again.

"How can this be? With this form and this beauty?" He touched her cheek, and she sighed. "How can you be alone?"

"I don't want to be with them. They're shallow and stupid. All they care about is what I look like. They want to show me off."

"And you do not wish to be shown off?"

Lacie glanced down and whispered, "I wish to be with you."

Cagliastro raised a wicked black brow at her. "There is a terrible price to pay."

She nodded, prepared for some mystical tribulation.

"I want the old Lacie back. The woman of the warm heart and full curves. I do not require that other men desire you. It is enough for me that I cannot think of my life without you. Can you pay that price, my love?"

***

"Who is that with Lacie, Mom?" Lacie's sister, Blythe, asked as the reception was winding down and her sister walked out the door with the handsome stranger she'd brought to the wedding.

"I'm not sure, honey, but they looked good together, didn't they?"

Blythe nodded. "I could swear she finally lost some weight."

Her mother laughed. "I don't think she cares, honey. I think she might have found what she was looking for."

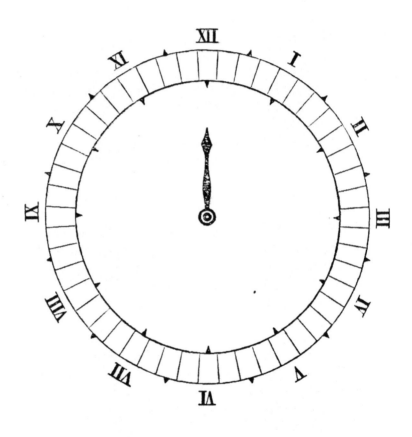

Fargan Rum

We've always loved Edgar Allan Poe, one of the great masters of suspense and a favorite author. While he's known for his mystery, suspense, and horror, not as many people think of him for his science fiction. But he often included scientific details in his stories and wrote about the limits and consequences of the technology of the day. "Fargan Rum" is our tribute to one of his stories, "Masque of the Red Death." We added a privateer—you can never go wrong with a good privateer.

So! You've found me at last. I've no notion of the time or the date. Perhaps it's only seemed an eternity that we've drifted here. Forever blackness does that to you. Out here, all things are relative. So often they are all an illusion.

No, don't touch that door. She's in there. Dormant, probably. Dreaming of this day, when she might be free again. Don't listen to her if she starts to beg. I've sealed the compartment, or you wouldn't be alive now. I've a mug of rum here, somewhere. It's Fargan rum, you know. Men have done foolish things to drink it. Hot, it soothes the soul. I'm afraid I've lost my taste for it now. I rarely thirst for anything anymore.

Let me tell you about myself. (I assume you're telepathic to understand me now.) I am Taylin. My ship is Taylin's Chance. We've been together longer than I care to recall. I am—I guess, I was—an independent pay the most. Rum, especially Fargan rum, is damn right expensive.

I picked up some medical supplies from Telfa Base and ran them to Ria when a plague broke out. I'm not sure how long ago. There wasn't much to it at first, but then it began to spread all over the planet.

No one knew what caused it—or worse, how to cure it. They tried everything. For my purposes, they paid top coin because of the danger. Plague, disaster, war—they were my specialties because I'd go where no one else dared to go. I was never afraid.

Until I met her.

She was waiting in the med tech's office when I brought in the supplies. Pale, fragile, with bones of a child and hair the color of sunrise. She looked at me with eyes that had more depth than I could comprehend. It was then I began to drown.

The plague was putrid. Rotting flesh and wasted minds. Hands that would never hold anything again gripped then slid off the blaster at my side. People begged to die. There was so much blood, and the stench of disease permeated everything.

It seemed hopeless to me, but the techs fought on valiantly, mostly giving comfort. Death was the only cure.

They told me that the girl would leave the planet with me. After quarantine, of course, to be sure we were both clean. I rarely carried passengers.

We boarded Chance together, and I showed her the spare cabin, not much more than a storeroom. She never said a word. Three days and nights we waited for clearance while I ran safety checks and counted supplies.

Mostly I was running low on my bootleg case of rum. Farga never legally allows it's prime source of income to leave the planet. But a few of us always managed to bring a little back. It was almost time to run back to Farga for anything else of value—just for the rum.

I was still carrying parts for mining machines on Mentar.

When I got clearance to leave Ria, I planned on going directly there. I finally had a reason to speak directly to her.

She opened the door at my knock, and I thought she looked paler than before.

"We leave Ria in only a short time," I told her. "Any special place you're going?"

"I have no name," she replied vaguely.

"I'm only going to a mining colony for a brief drop. You're welcome to stay on till Farga."

Her smile was slight. "You are very kind."

We left Ria and the plague just after I spoke to her. She hadn't mentioned credits or coins, but I figured that she had to know that there was no free ride.

Mentar came up quickly. Chance was no slouch when there was money to be made. She came out of her cabin as we approached the planet and received permission to land.

"The mining colony?" She gestured towards the green gray plaid of the world on the viewing screen.

"Mentar," I nodded. "Not a pretty place, but they supply ore for half the system."

She sat next to me in the vacant chair while we landed. We were greeted by the commander general of the company. But when I turned to ask her if she wanted a breath of planet air, she was gone.

The mining parts were unloaded without my supervision. I glanced around quickly for the girl, knowing she could not stay on Mentar, a planet full of men. I felt responsible for bringing her there. It would be my neck in the vice when she showed up there alone.

In the end, there was no reason for concern. She returned just as Chance was finished unloading. I had traded a fine, old bottle of rum for a meal not dried or flaked. The commander drove a hard bargain.

She came through the door, slightly dirty, her hair disheveled, a bright flush rising on her cheeks. She was breathing hard, and her eyes were strangely bright.

"Are you well?" I asked, worried about the plague.

"I am very well," she enunciated clearly, her voice a husky growl. "Where next, Taylin?"

"Farga," I answered, amazed at the change in her. Gone was the lost, wild look, the air of fragility. She seemed suddenly to have become a woman, strong and ripe for plunder. Her hair seemed to have deepened in color, now almost a royal shade of rose.

My blood raced at the sight of her. "About the fee for your ride to Farga."

"Perhaps we can come to an understanding." She came toward me, fairly pulsing with life and heat. She wound her arms around my neck, and my head swam. My breathing seemed to stop, while my heart pounded thunderously. She'd be holding me up by the time she kissed me.

I laughed at my weakness. But there was nothing amusing about her possession of me. She sucked the breath from my lungs and left me gasping while her teeth shredded my skin. I cried out in pleasure and pain while she reduced me to a shivering, sobbing heap.

"My ride for your life, Taylin," she hissed near my ear.

I agreed, hating her yet begging her to use me again and again. I looked into her eyes and knew terror deeper than my soul.

"Who are you?" I whispered in awe.

"Do you not recognize me, Taylin? I can be your death. Or I can be your life."

"I want to live!" I cried out as white hot agony shot through me at her touch.

"You will," she acceded, moving away from me. "We go to Farga. Then to Telfa."

I nursed a mug of hot rum in a tiny taverna frequented by independents. There was a restless, wary look to them that set the atmosphere on edge. There was talk of plague, of death and horror. Somehow, despite strict quarantine, the bloody plague had spread from Ria to Mentar.

I drank deeply and cringed in my corner. She had been to both places. She had left me earlier that day as the sun rose over the only city on Farga, my body aching, my hand with a fine tremor that forced me to hold the mug with both hands. What was she doing on those crowded streets while I sat in terror of her return?

The door opened, and a whistling wind jerked it back with a bang that left all those hardy souls quivering. Everyone looked up.

She was framed in the doorway by the fading sunlight, her hair blood red, streaming wildly around her. I felt her eyes search for and find me among the lost souls in that crowd. A thrill of fear, excitement, and arousal gripped me, hot and cold at once. I stood, not really of my own will, when she beckoned. It was time to leave.

As I reached the door, a man to my left put up his hand to wipe the sweat of fear from his brow. His hand came away sickeningly red. His eyes bulged, and he screamed.

Instances of plague had already been reported when we requested permission to leave Farga. Quarantine would be scrupulously observed before the entire system was infected.

"Leave now," she commanded as we waited for word from Fargan authorities.

I pressed the starter switch. Chance's engines throbbed around us. Control reminded us that we had not been given permission to leave the planet. But we were up and gone from Fargan airspace before a second, more strident command to halt could be issued.

"You're doing that!" I looked at my companion as we entered the familiar exchange route between Farga and Telfa. "You're bringing the plague. You're a carrier, aren't you?"

The truth had dawned too late to help Farga, but Telfa could be saved.

"I am death for some." She shrugged carelessly then slid her arms around my neck. "But I am life for you. Without me, you will die as surely as the others."

"What are you saying? If you gave them the plague, why not me?" I demanded, trying to move away from her embrace.

She scraped her fingernail across my cheek, drawing a glistening drop of blood on the tip of her finger, which she licked at delicately and smiled.

"You please me, Taylin. I am immune. I have shared my immunity with you. But it is only temporary for as long as I am with you. If I leave, if you displease me, then you die. Like the others. Maybe a little longer, a little harder."

She kissed me then. Truly the kiss of death. She was soft beneath me, and my mind exploded in an agony of light and passion. I was already dying with her silken hair wrapped around my face.

By lying I knew I could get us down on Telfa, despite the plague.

And I knew I would.

How could I let all those people on beautiful, green Telfa die? I was alive, I reasoned. If I stalled for time, maybe I'd find a way to stop her without murdering myself. I used all of these reasons for setting down on the far eastern side.

The truth was that I was scared—heart throbbing, gut rending. I didn't know what else to do.

She smiled and waved as she descended from the ship to the landing area. So confident, so damn certain that I would not leave her there. I looked again, but she was lost in the fast-moving crowd.

"How long do you think she'll let you live?" a voice that rasped like old machinery asked of me.

I turned to face an old man, barely standing upright, his grizzled head bent towards me. His eyes were keen in his much-lined face. He knew the truth.

"How long?" he asked again when I made no reply. "While she murders millions of innocents, you worry about your own life, which is forfeit already."

"How do you know?" I demanded. "You can't judge me

or my actions."

The battered body trembled with strong emotion. "I have seen her kind before—a mutant strain that was thought to be extinct long ago. She feeds on the pain, the suffering. How long, I ask, are you prepared to be half alive before you save the rest of us?"

"I'm no hero, old man. I'll take whatever time I can, and to hell with the rest."

"Bide your time, boy, then seal her off from what's left of humanity." He wandered to the doorway. "Real death is far less painful."

She came back to the ship, eyes glazed, breasts heaving as though she'd been with a lover. She was unbelievably, hideously, beautiful.

I looked at her, and I knew that the old man had spoken the truth.

"Back from your trip to the grave?" I asked quickly.

She looked at me calmly. "I am tired, Taylin. We are ready to leave now."

"Surely," I agreed. "Where does My Lady wish to destroy next?"

"That is enough. I am ready to go now, Taylin!" Her voice shook slightly with beginning anger. I felt an answering tremor of fear.

Chance lifted off smoothly. I looked out at lush, dying Telfa and wondered if they knew yet. I saluted her with a taste of rum. We had both seen the best of this life. When we reached the upper atmosphere, I looked at the familiar patterns that the ship's control requested for guidance.

"Next in line seems to be Salim 3," she commented from where she stood beside me.

I punched overdrive and felt the pull of power as Chance surged forward into the outer reaches instead of following the expected route. My head pounded with the exertion. My eyes were dry, my mind quite lucid. When we faced the blackness of full space, I hit the final red button on the console.

Not so bad, I considered. All independents go out this way.

"What are you doing?" she queried, glancing at the control board. A flutter of sparks and the smell of acrid fumes accompanied her words. "Taylin!"

"Too late," I laughed. "There's nothing left to do now."

"What have you done?" She pushed me aside as though I were an obnoxious insect. "You will destroy us!"

"That's the general idea, my love," I countered from the floor, tasting blood in my mouth. "It can't be undone."

"No!" she shrieked, frantically hitting buttons to no avail. We were adrift in space, hopefully forever. I sat in the pilot's chair and faced the screen. Fear was gone then. What was left to fear past death itself?

"Taylin, you fool!" she screamed. "You will die, you know. I will not save you. You will die horribly, begging for mercy."

I looked at her, feeling numb yet content. "The beauty of it is that I don't go alone."

She hit me again then ran hysterically through the ship. When she reached the cargo area, I calmly kicked the heavy door closed then sealed it shut with my blaster.

Then I waited.

Her wails and screams subsided eventually into moans and calls for mercy. She stirred my pity as well as my passion, but there was no going back. She was entombed, and I was damned. It was a fitting end.

I drank heavily of my meager stock of rum then I slept. I'm not certain how long. I awoke with my body burning and my teeth trembling with cold. Blood dripped from my forehead. I thought I heard her laughter.

Sometime later, I thought of my blaster again. There was no reason to prolong the agony, after all. I reached for it on the control console, but my hands, scarcely more than skeletal claws, could not use its delicate firing mechanism.

So I was trapped here. Until now.

Now, take my rum; I will never enjoy its pleasures again.

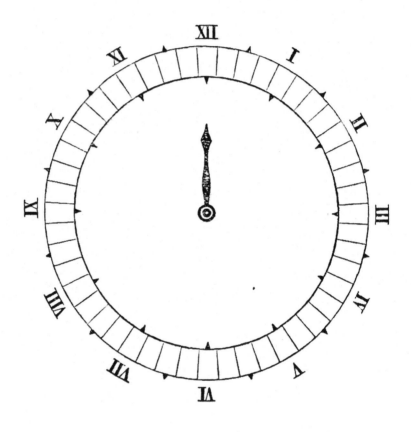

One With The Darkness

A string of mysterious deaths in the old South sparks rumors of blasphemy and suicide. One brave soul resists the darkness, but is her love strong enough? Years before Stella meets Eric, the ghost in the Sweet Pepper Fire Brigade series, other spirits haunt the long, lonely nights.

When I was a child, there was a woman who lived in our well. I was eight before I realized that she was dead.

Every day, my mother would send me out to get water. I would speak to the woman, and she would speak back to me. I never thought to question how she got there. Or how she could live in that cold, dark place. I would politely wish her a good morning, and she would politely whisper the same.

When I was eight, a neighbor boy heard me speaking to her. "Who're you talkin' to?"

I looked at him as if he were as stupid and irritating as anything could ever be. "The woman who lives in the well."

He laughed. Then he sobered as he continued to stare at my face. He became a sullen, sickly shade of white and green. "Ain't no woman in that well!"

"You don't think so?" I demanded. "Come see."

I didn't see her reach for him. I did see him strain to look into those dark depths. He was there one moment in his blue jeans and his red bandana. Then he was gone. I looked down the well after him but I couldn't see him.

"Where are you?" I whispered.

"Gone," the woman in the well whispered back to me.

I ran back to the house and got Ma. She dried her hands on her apron and came out after me. Together, we looked into the well. This time, he was there, face down in the water. Ma screamed and ran back to the house.

The woman in the well smiled at me.

They came with torches that night and took the well apart, stone by stone. Ma held me tight when they looked at me while they brought out the boy's body. He was more sickly pale and green than before. He seemed to be looking at me. I hid my eyes in Ma's dress.

They found bones at the bottom of the well. They took them out and crushed them under their feet then the parson came and buried what was left in the road. He cursed the bones and spat upon them. I never talked to the lady again. We left there soon after.

I only tell you this because it explains why I didn't think it was unusual to have a man outside my bedroom window.

The first time I saw him, he was standing in the shade of an old oak tree. The moss hanging from the thick branches made it hard to tell he was there. I turned my head this way and that, and I realized that I could barely make out his form. He was tall, more shadow than substance. He was looking at my window. I quickly turned out the light.

At first, I thought it might be my husband's shade. He'd been killed in the war. I'd gotten the telegram just a few weeks before. I thought he might be coming back to see me. I thought about running down to him. Something held me back.

Instead, I watched and waited to see what he would do next. For seven nights, he waited in the darkness and the moss. I looked at him from behind the curtain in my room. I never saw his face.

I wasn't afraid. Just cautious. It never paid to embrace the night without knowing the truth.

On the eighth night, I awoke to see him outside my window—no mean feat, since my window was twenty feet from the ground. His face was pale, so pale. The shadows created lines in his cheeks. His eyes were black coals that burned into my soul. I felt him in every fiber of my being.

"Come to me," he said in a voice of unearthly beauty. "I need you."

"No," I replied firmly. "Leave me."

"Come to me," he said. "You need me."

I got up in the chill of the night and closed the window against him. I pulled the shade down so I couldn't see his face. But I couldn't stop him from speaking.

"I can give you everything." His voice was a silky promise. "I ask for nothing in return."

I refused to answer. I had to keep my lips tightly shut to keep the words from coming from my lips. It felt like he was inside of my brain, the words echoing and enticing.

"Let me kiss you. Let me hold you to me. I can show you delights you have never dreamed. Your breasts already ache for my mouth."

I could feel my breasts tighten at his words. Their peaks stood out against the fine cloth of my night gown.

"Your body is so warm. You can feel me inside of you, hot and hard. Let me love you. You want me. Don't deny me. Don't deny yourself."

I shifted in bed, refusing to acknowledge what his words did to me. I was hot and shaking with need, with desire. He continued to speak to me in a voice of honey that spread through me. I couldn't stop him. I couldn't stop the effect his words had on me. I held on to the bedclothes with grasping fingers.

It was as though my body dragged me off the bed and across the floor. It was no conscious act that made me put my hands on the windowsill to open the window. I needed him. I wanted him. Nothing could stop me from having what he promised. A dark paradise was in his voice. Promises of rapture thrilled me and left me barely able to breathe.

Then the rooster crowed. I pulled open the shade, but he was gone with the first fingers of light. Wearily, I collapsed into my bed and slept through most of the day, his words still echoing through me.

At noon, Mrs. Fannie Albright came to call. She brought her knitting, her rolling eyes, and a queer tale. An acquaintance of ours, who had also lost her husband, was found dead in her yard. Still in her night gown, she had such a look of terror on her face that the sheriff called the minister to say some words over her body right then and there.

"And you know there was that woman the next county over who was found the same way, 'cept she was on her porch," Fannie reminded me.

"That's right." I recalled the story. The woman had also been recently widowed.

"There's something dark going on. Mark my words."

"Have you heard from Daniel?" I asked about her husband, who like mine, was fighting for the cause.

"Not for three months. I pray to God that he is well."

"I've heard that the tide is against us since Atlanta. I fear the days of our glorious cause are at hand."

Fannie rolled her eyes. "I pray you are wrong and that you will not speak so before me again. We must prevail, or everything is lost. Do you suppose the Yankees will be content in only burning Atlanta? There will be nothing left of any of us if we lose."

I didn't dare disagree. The war had taken its sure and awful toll. Already everything good had been taken from us. Burning the rest of us out of our homes could surely make it no worse.

She left after tea, chamomile, which I had in the garden since I could afford nothing else. A weary soldier came soon after, limping to my door, his once proud uniform in tatters. I asked him in and gave him food. He ate greedily, stuffing his gaunt frame with what meager food I had to offer.

"What news is there from the war?"

"None good," he told me quietly. There were terrible ghosts in his eyes that haunted him from the things he'd seen and done. "I have come back with a list of the dead from Colonel Scott."

He pulled out a greasy, matted correspondence.

I looked at the missive and choked when I read Captain Albright's name. My poor, sweet friend had also lost her husband.

"The Yankees will have put us down in another month," the soldier told me. "There is nothing more to win. There is only the surrender."

He left me about sunset. I watched him limp down the road then glanced at the oak tree and shivered. Night was coming. I closed and barred the door.

Refusing to give that creature another chance to call to me, I slept in another bedroom in the empty house. The night was long and silent, but I did not hear his voice again.

In the morning, I awakened, refreshed and glad that I had put that dark soul away from me. I took my only horse, a skinny nag too old for the soldiers to steal, and I went to comfort Fannie. Her farm was only a few miles away. I thought about the lost lives and lost hope that had accompanied our glorious cause. Nothing we could have gained was worth what we had lost.

Where would we go from here? I wondered as I passed an empty farm house and an untilled field. How would we survive?

I reached Fannie's home and left my horse at the hitching post. I called to her as I walked into her house. There was no reply. I thought about that dark voice calling to me. I thought about those other widows who had not had the strength to stay away.

"Fannie?" I called, starting to run. My heart raced in my bosom, and fear blossomed like unholy flowers in my mind. "Fannie!"

I found her in the back garden. She was lying in a shallow pool of water.

A cold-eyed angel looked down at her from the fountain. Her eyes were open. Fear etched her face and hollowed her gaze.

She was dead without a mark on her.

I sat beside her for a long time, thinking about the creature that had come to prey on us in our time of suffering and grief. Somehow, it knew when our husbands died. Perhaps it had followed the news from the battlefield.

"I shall not allow him to steal another soul, Fannie," I promised as I held her ice cold hand. "I swear this on your dying breath!"

When I went to town and got the sheriff, he told me that he figured it was grief and loss that was taking the widows. Somehow, they were taking their own lives. Poison or a broken heart had killed them. There had been five in the past month.

I didn't argue with him, though I knew better. My mind was seething with plans for how I would rid us of this creature.

Yet, everything I knew couldn't help me. I had felt his pull that first night. If there had been five minutes more before sunrise, I would already be dead. I resisted him, but it had only given me one more day.

And it had cost Fannie her life.

I knew he would be back at my window that night. I understood that I didn't know how to fight him. Terrified to see the sky begin to darken, I hurried home. I did not want to meet the apparition on the road.

Clearly, he was powerful but could not come into the house. All of his victims had been found outside.

Barely having time to stable the old nag before night swept its dark hand across the land, I shut and bolted the door. I stood with my back against the thick portal, panting with exertion and wondering what to do next. With no plan in mind and the horror of the night before me, I crouched in a chair, shuddering in anticipation.

I must have fallen asleep because I heard his voice from my dream. I was dreaming about Peter, my husband. Peter, who had looked so dashing in his uniform.

He hadn't wanted to go and leave me. He was a man of books and learning, not a soldier. They had conscripted him, and he had made the best of it. It had been the war or a filthy prison. He had kissed me goodbye and gone off to die in the hills of Tennessee.

Half asleep, I walked to the door and opened it. The night was dark, and the wind sighed through the tree tops. There was no moon and no owls or doves crying from the trees.

"You need me," he whispered to me from the darkness. "You are so alone."

I shook my head and forced my feet to stay where they were—inside the threshold. I could not, for the love of God or man, close the door against him. "You will kill me."

"No, I only want to love you, to have you love me."

"Is that what you did with Fannie Albright? Did you love her until she died?"

"I am only here for you," he promised me. "I know that you are lonely. I know that your heart aches for your loss. Let me love you. I can take away the pain."

"I will not come to you," I told him, though the words were thick as syrup trying to come out of my mouth. "I will not let you have my soul."

"I can be... anyone... for you." He stood before me suddenly, wearing Peter's face.

"That is the cruelest ruse of all," I told him angrily. "You will never be my husband! I love Peter. Nothing that you are can change that. No magic can make me accept you as my love."

"Not magic," he said quietly, holding out his arms to me. "Only love. Long nights of my kisses and my warmth beside you. Sweet, sweet desire that I offer you. You are so alone. So afraid. Let me hold you. Let me touch you."

His voice was like the warmest summer breeze sweeping across my face. It was as gentle as sunshine and as sweet as perfume. It was intoxicating.

I was lightheaded and nearly drunk with it. There was no tomorrow. No fear.

There was only the creature, looking like my own dear Peter, standing before me with his arms outstretched. I wanted to step into those sheltering arms almost more than I wanted my life. I wanted to feel his lips on mine and guide his hands on my body. I wanted him to love me, to forget the terrifying future and the sadness that had come to live in my soul.

The yes spilled out of my lips before I could stop it. My foot hovered on the step that would take me out the door to him. I crossed an invisible boundary that had protected me.

He swept me into his arms and pressed me against his unholy flesh. I was smothered in darkness. He put his mouth to mine. His lips tasted of wine, but they were cold. His hands touched me everywhere. Again and again, I cried out in helpless ecstasy. There was no force, only a complete surrender of body and spirit. I knew that he would kill me, but I could not stop him.

As he loved me, a tear slid down my cheek. Then another followed. My breath came in ragged throes. My heart pounded in my chest. I closed my eyes, knowing the end was near.

I thought about Peter and how much I loved him. I thought about the children we had planned to have and the life we had wanted to share. I saw him smile at me and felt his caress in the early summer heat. I heard his voice and smiled at his laughter.

He would always be a part of me. Death couldn't take him from me. The creature who was laying claim to my body could not keep me from dreaming of him.

The dark creature moved away from me. "You think only of him."

I wanted to cry out for the creature's touch, but I pushed down those dark urges. "Yes."

"Even though he is gone and you will not see him again in heaven or hell?"

"I will die gladly with his name on my lips."

He stroked his hand down my cheek, and I shuddered with wanting him. "What makes you different?"

I paused and considered. I knew the answer. "Even though I can't stop my body from dying to be with you, even though you steal my soul, you shall not have my love. It will always belong to Peter."

"I could take you now."

I thrilled to think of it, but I held on to whatever bit of self-control I possessed. "I know."

"Why do you resist?"

"For the love of him." I dared to look into those terrible eyes. "What does it matter?"

"In my arms, women forget. In their loneliness and grief, they long to forget. I offer a relief from memory and pain. None resist."

"I do not want to forget. I grieve gladly. Peter will always be in my heart."

He touched me again. I closed my eyes on the pleasure it brought me. When I opened them again, he was gone. My knees felt suddenly weak, and my stomach lurched up in my throat. I leaned across the porch rail and vomited what little was in my stomach.

He was gone. I sensed, I don't know how, that he would not return to trouble me. My vow to Fannie weighed heavily on my conscience until I realized that I could not have killed the creature. I was amazed to be alive.

I sat on the porch all through the long night. In the clear pink light of morning, a figure moved down the road from a long way off. He was walking straight and proud. His uniform was ragged, and his hat was gone. The golden sun glinted off his golden hair.

Peter!

In an instant, I was on my feet and running down the dew-dampened road to meet him. I lost my shawl and my shoes, but I never slowed. My hair cascaded down on my shoulders, but I didn't stop to pin it.

He caught me in his arms. I looked at him eagerly, seeing the terrible blow on his head that still had not healed, the blood and dust on his gray uniform. He kissed me, and I knew such fierce joy that I cried aloud at it.

"I love you," he said in his old way. "I will never leave you again."

"They said you were dead," I lamented, tears streaming down my face. "They said—"

"Shh." He gently covered my lips with his fingers. "I'm here for you as long as I am in your heart."

I looked at him, hearing his strange words. It was Peter, my beloved Peter. That he should be there after suffering a death blow like the one to his head was a miracle. That he should be there—

I cannot say that I didn't know, that I didn't guess the truth. Yet I looked at him and did not question. In a way, I kept my vow to Fannie because no other widows died in that terrible way, yet there were many that last year of the war that lamented the loss of their husbands. And if sometimes, I see the darkness in him, still he has been a good and faithful husband. He has been everything that Peter could have been to me and more.

For in the dark stretches of the night, he comes to me. His voice is like the breeze, and his mouth is like dark wine. He touches me, and the velvet of the summer cloak falls across me. His eyes burn into mine, and we become one with the darkness.

Cold Karma

Sometimes plots come to writers from the strangest places. Like we mentioned about Edgar Allan Poe earlier, we've often thought about the boundaries of technology and what it could lead to. "Cold Karma" came about in a discussion about cryogenics, like the urban legend of Walt Disney's head being frozen, in storage somewhere underneath Disneyland. But what makes this story interesting to us isn't the technology but how the story reflects part of the human condition—the desire to stay alive and the willingness to do almost anything to make that happen.

"Billy," he said, standing resolutely. "I think it's time."

"Time, Uncle Marcus?" his nephew asked, glancing up at his uncle curiously.

"Time for you to learn the truth, Billy," Marcus Holder flexed his shoulders in his five-hundred-dollar business suit. He was a big man, hard to fit, with powerful arms and a thick neck.

Billy pushed his glasses back on his nose and stood up slowly as his uncle came around the Cherrywood desk. "I don't think I understand, Uncle Marcus."

"You will, boy. Let's go for a ride."

The black Bentley was brought around to the street entrance to the Holder Building. The chauffeur nodded, pulled at his gray cap as the two men went quickly from the doorway into the dark interior of the car.

"The cryo lab," Marcus told the chauffeur, liking the deference in the young man's eyes. A man should know his place—not necessarily stay there but at least understand where he stood.

The elder Holding turned to the man who reminded him so much of himself. He wished his brother could have been there to see the boy—tall and thin like Mikey Holding had been but with intelligence and ambition in his dark eyes. Like Marcus himself. There was a resolution to the boy, a determined patience that wore down any resistance in his path.

"I want you to know the truth about the Holder money," Marcus said finally. He was pleased to see a sharpening in the boy's eyes.

Billy shrugged, leaned back in the dark upholstery. "What's to know? You and Dad struck it rich in the cryo business back in the eighties."

"That's true enough," Marcus agreed, "but there's more. It's time, Billy. You should know. With Mikey gone, you're my only family. Someday, you'll have to take care of it. Better to learn now."

Mikey Holder's death, twenty years before, had been needless and tragic. Marcus had adopted his brother's only child, raising him as his own. Billy's mother had died at his birth, his father when he was ten. Marcus Holder was the only father he could actually recall.

The Bentley pulled up smoothly in front of the squat, ugly cryo lab. The gray cinder block walls, windowless and dirty, were a remote world away from the plush, modern, glass and titanium of the Holder Building.

"I'll call you when I want you to come back," Marcus told the chauffeur.

"How old is this place?" Billy wondered, scuffing his foot on the cracked and overgrown sidewalk going to the door.

"Probably from back in the late sixties when cryo first started. This is where your father and I first started working. This is where it all is."

Billy looked at his uncle's intent face, knowing the man never joked about money.

"I'm afraid I don't get it."

"You will." Marcus laughed, clapping him on the back. "Come on."

The security was elaborate. There were five entrances to the building, each with an individual alarm and scanning device. Once a door was open, lasers were triggered, reacting to infrared heat scanners. Only a fast move and knowledge of the next security code could save a severely burned limb.

"Now!" Marcus opened the sealed door into the heart of the lab. The door was more than a foot thick, but it slid back lightly at the proper sequence of lights on the front panel.

The lab was dark, but the lights responded to voice command. Computers flickered to life around them as Marcus Holder removed his coat. "Look around you, boy. It's all here."

"Sir?"

"The power, the money—it's all right here."

Billy looked around at the gleaming cryo equipment. Most were older models, tubes and cylinders, some full size, some only half a meter high.

"You want me to learn to freeze people?" the young man asked, perplexed.

Marcus laughed, a hollow sound in the sterile room. "There was never any money in that stuff. Me and Mikey, we thought there was to begin with. How could you go wrong? No one wants to die. People would pay anything to stay alive or for the remote chance that they might be able to come back later."

Billy followed him as he started to walk through the lab. "So you charged them twenty-thousand for their heads to be frozen, fifty-thousand for their bodies. It built up. But there's still no way to bring them back."

"That never really mattered, did it?" Marcus asked confidently. "After all, we were talking years in the future. After we'd made our money and were gone."

"But—"

"It was small potatoes to begin with, mostly machos and pathetic losers. I didn't see how we could make anything. The equipment was expensive to maintain. The government kept us in court until legal fees threatened to close us down."

"Then what?" Billy asked.

"Your father was working night and day trying to find a way to bring them back. He thought it would become more popular, easier to defend. Most of the things wrong with them were curable within ten years."

They stopped in front of a workstation covered in all manner of scientific equipment that Billy didn't really understand. "But he never found a way. No one ever has, even now. The ones they bring back are like zombies."

"That's right. But your father found something better. Something that put us where we are today." Marcus stepped to a small cylinder and switched a light that dimly lit the interior. It was not dissimilar from looking into an aquarium. Thick gel surrounded something that looked back at them.

Billy moved a step back from it. The pale blue eyes blinked slowly, and the mouth moved—open and close, open and close. "What the hell is it?"

"Not it. He. Carl Mason." Marcus tapped on the glass at the face.

"Can it—he see us?" Billy moved closer.

"Sure. Your father came up with this gel. I don't know why it works, but as long as the head stays in it, Carl is alive."

"Just the head?"

"It wouldn't work for the whole body. We lost a few of them trying. But, Billy, this is it."

"What?" He looked away with an effort from the

grotesque human yet nonhuman face.

"Carl Mason—no family, no friends. Clinically dead since 1970. He left his fortune in a bank account to be retrieved when he came back."

He walked to another cylinder and flicked on a light. "Sandra Rhodes, dead since 1992. No family, no friends. One hundred-million dollars in a closed account."

A light came on in Billy's eyes. "You found a way to access it?"

"Exactly. When retinal scans became the banking ID, it all started to click in my head. I didn't understand how it kept them alive, but I understood this—" He returned to the first cylinder. "Open your eyes, Carl. Open them, or you know I'll pull the plug."

The eyes opened slowly behind the glass.

"Poor bastard still wants to live." Marcus smiled and picked up a computer scanner from the table next to them. With one hand, he punched in a banking ID number that corresponded to Carl Mason.

"Retinal scan required for access to account J4720," the computer informed him coldly.

Marcus raised the scanner to the glass closest to Carl's face. It took only an instant.

"Retinal scan complete. Access permitted."

"You see? The gel even helps by conducting the scan through it better than if it was you or me out here." Marcus looked at his nephew triumphantly. "Now do you see? I have over a hundred people here. So long as they survive, we prosper."

"My father was so close." Billy shook his head. "He might have been able to do the whole process."

Marcus put down the computer scanner and walked to the cylinder that held Sandra Rhodes. It showed a gray-green head, her eyes staring out at them.

"It's all here for us. I wish your father could have shared it. He would've wanted you to be a part of it." He switched off the light in the Rhodes cylinder, turning to look at the rest of the shiny, silver tubes. "You've been like a son to me. You're all the family I have left."

"There's just one thing, Uncle Marcus," Billy said.

Marcus started to turn then felt a blow to his head, crying out as he slid to the floor. He saw the bright lights in the ceiling and felt the cold of the concrete floor on his back. Then his eyes closed, and the light faded.

* * *

"Uncle Marcus? Uncle Marcus, can you hear me?"

Marcus Holder blinked in the light. His mouth opened, and something cold flowed onto his tongue.

"I'm glad you're awake," Billy said, relief in his voice. "I thought you were dead."

Marcus tried to speak, but no words came.

"Just rest. You'll be fine. I'm glad you felt you could tell me this finally. I knew there was something, but I couldn't put my finger on it. But you're right. I can handle it all. My father would have wanted this. He wouldn't have wanted you to die right away, even though you killed him quickly."

Marcus Holder's eyes flew open wide. His mouth worked in silent horror, his scream sounding only in his mind.

"Did you think I forgot? Or did you think I didn't know? You were never like a father to me. You killed my father."

Billy lifted the scanning pen from the computer desk at his side.

"Open wide, Uncle Marcus. I want to continue my father's research, and it's going to take a lot of money."

Alice in Renaissance Were-Land

What makes a great battle at the Renaissance Faire Village and Marketplace? A strong enemy, a sound strategy, and a couple of shape-shifters. Even though we love Jessie and Chase, it was fun to write about a character who isn't the center of attention in the novels. Wait until you see what we do tomorrow night!

Lady Alice swung her sword, chopping through the first line of zombies that had surrounded Renaissance Faire Village. The moonlight glinted silver on her blood-stained blade. She moved with ease and deftness – never flinching from the grizzly task. She knew if she didn't reach the inner square before midnight, the village would be lost.

Beside her fought an eight-foot werewolf, recently chained. Part of the chain still swung from his neck. He was savage, unstoppable—yet even he appeared to be tiring.

"We need a miracle," she said during a lull in the battle. Her partner snarled but didn't reply. The transformation process from the burly sword maker in the village was too intense to go through for the sake of mere conversation.

The assault on the village had begun at moonrise. Zombies had been ensorcelled to attack the residents who lived here. At midnight, that same sorcery would carry the village into a black dimension from which there was no escape. Lady Alice could think of nothing worse.

A group of vampires were somewhere inside the village, fighting for their lives too, no doubt. She cleaned her sword, looked at her companion licking the blood from his fur, and got ready for the next onslaught. She hated fighting zombies. They had no finesse, no skill to match hers against. Better to pit her against demons that could at least make polite conversation while trying to kill her.

The moonlight fluttered, making her look toward the skies. A dragon, one of the biggest she'd ever seen, was swooping close to her. Was he friend or foe? So far, the enchantment had taken only the lowest of the undead—the brainless creatures—but it was always possible it could spread.

The dragon's scales gleamed in the moonlight. The pale green-blue looked like sunlight on the ocean. The creature was so large that it blocked out the oncoming pack of zombies behind it. Luminescence gleamed at its mouth. Lady Alice knew what that meant and shielded herself from the fiery spew as the dragon released its fury on the zombies.

Ah, fire, she thought. Better than a blade for zombies, since there was nothing left to clean up. Of course, there was the acrid smell of burning flesh and hair. The dragon seemed to answer her question about whose side it was on.

Even as she let down her guard for a moment, the dragon made its transformation into a man. He was naked, of course, as was usually the case with were-dragons.

"Greetings, Lady Alice." He bowed to her with no notion of awkwardness about his naked, muscular body, still tinged with green luminescence. "I have news from the castle."

"How goes the battle then, dragon?"

"The vampire line has held. The king and queen are safe. Except for a few pesky zombies, the battle is won—in our favor. The king hails your brilliant strategy."

"Good news, Sir Dragon!"

"The werewolves will slay what remains," he said.

"Let's go home. It's been a long night."

Lady Alice sheathed her blade. "I hope the visitors enjoyed the battle. I think I sprained my wrist. Those were some damn big zombies! And they just kept coming."

"All in a night's work at Renaissance Village and Marketplace." The man transformed back into the dragon. "I promise to lick your every wound, my lady. You should be fine by morning."

"A bath first, I think, my sweet dragon prince." She climbed on his back. He was exceedingly warm to the touch as she straddled him. His heat was a balm to her sore muscles. "And tomorrow, I am going shopping for a new outfit. Maybe a new blade as well. I can only be expected to perform at my best if properly garbed and weaponed."

"Your wish, as they say, is my command, my lady love. Tomorrow is another day—another battle for the glory of Renaissance Village."

"Ghouls tomorrow night, right?"

"I haven't seen the new schedule yet." He rose on huge wings that beat mightily at the cool night air. "To the east!"

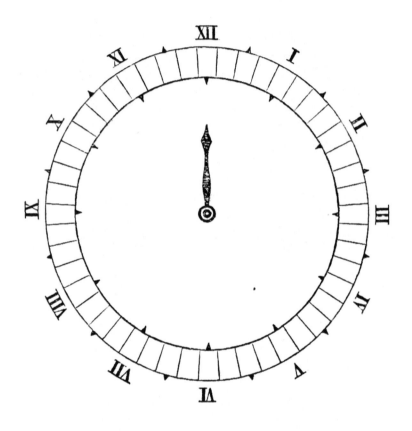

Gone By Midnight

Dedicated to the memory of Joyce's mother, Joan

One of the questions we hear the most from readers is whether we write about our lives in our books. Most of the time the answer is no, other than little things like going to the coffee shop or naming a character after someone we know. But this story is close to our family's hearts. Joyce's mother moved away from her family when she got married and wasn't able to make it back before her own mother passed away. This story was born of that heartache. Some of the events of the story are real, and some are imagined. We'll leave it up to you to decide which is which.

I am gone by midnight. The train pulls slowly from the empty station. The ticket clerk wearily closes his lighted window.

"Where are we going?" Molly asks me.

"To see Grandma," I tell her.

"Isn't Daddy coming with us?"

It's an innocent question, one that makes sense to a five-year-old girl. I smooth down her blue jeans over her little, pink socks. "Not this time, honey. Let's try and get some sleep. It's going to be a long trip."

I hold her close to me on the worn, brown seat. The train is darkened for the sleeping passengers. The noise from the wheels is steady, with the bump, bump, bump of places where the rails are joined. Conversation whispers from one corner of the car, the sound of snoring from another. I look out at the lights in the sleeping towns we pass and wish I were home.

Not the house that I've shared with Bobby for the past ten years. That place of misery and heartache isn't home to me. Molly is the only thing good that came from that union. She is the only thing I brought away from it, besides the tattered remnants of my dignity. I didn't even stop to pack a suitcase after he hit me this time.

How many times had that been my downfall? Wasn't he sweet as peaches when he wasn't drinking and his fists didn't fly at me? Couldn't he beg and cry when he saw I meant to leave him?

This time was different. It was hard to explain how. It was something in Molly's eyes when he hit me. I wasn't looking at him. I was looking at our daughter and seeing her grow up, watching as her daddy beat her mommy. I hardly felt the blows he rained on me, though they closed my eye and split my lip. I was only thinking of my Molly.

When it was over, I didn't cry. The tears were gone. I sat in the corner and waited until he passed out. When I heard his heavy snoring, I took Molly's hand. We quietly put on our coats and gloves. I took all the money from Bobby's wallet and his drinking stash. Then we walked out the door.

It was so easy. I was afraid at first that it was a trick. I looked back over my shoulder until we got to the train station then again as we boarded the train.

"Two for Charleston," the conductor said as he clipped our ticket. "That's a long way."

I smiled but couldn't answer. I wished he'd hurry. I prayed he'd hurry. I expected to be caught at any moment. But we got on the train, and we took our seats.

Bobby didn't find us. We are safe. Will he come after us? Only time will tell.

But we'll be home.

The notion sings through my heart. After ten years, I am free. And I'm going home.

I was just fifteen when I last saw my family. Mama begged me not to marry the handsome sailor who'd taken me out and showed me a good time. She said he was selfish and mean. I only saw a way to leave home.

There were seven of us in that two-bedroom house my father had built with his hard, rough hands—no inside toilet.

No chance to ever do better.

It was hot in the summer and cold in the winter. I wanted so much more.

So I lied. I told her that I was pregnant. She slapped me. It didn't hurt so much as the look in her eyes. She got out her Bible and told me to do what I wanted. I wasn't welcome there anymore.

It cut me at first. Then I realized I had what I wanted. I was out of that house, and I was going to marry a handsome, young sailor with a good family in Chicago. I was going to have a house of my own and a car to drive. I was going to have nice clothes and a big diamond on my hand.

Now I had all those things. And a husband who drank until he couldn't bear to see my face.

It wasn't so bad until Molly was born. After that, Bobby began hitting me hard. He knocked out two of my teeth and fractured my jaw. I didn't know what to do. He said he'd take Molly away. He swore he loved me and he'd change if I gave him time.

I called my daddy, but he said Mama wouldn't come to the phone.

"You made your bed," he quoted her to me. "Now you'll lie in it."

I didn't know what to do. I almost resigned myself to enduring this hellish life. Then Mama called me one night. She told me she loved me and she wanted me to come home. She said she'd been sick and she didn't know how bad it was. I cried until I had no breath for my sobs to go on. I promised her that I would come right away.

That's where the fight started. Bobby told me it was stupid to go back to Charleston after ten years. I'd gone that long without seeing my family; I didn't need to go now.

I begged him on my knees. I pleaded with him to let me go. Mama had never seen Molly. It might be her last chance. He started beating me.

* * *

Molly moans a little beside me, and I open my eyes. We have transferred trains for the last time. A whole day has gone. It is another night.

I pick her up in my arms and cradle her close to me. I can smell the shampoo in her hair. She isn't a little girl, and it's not long before my arms are aching. But every time I try to put her back in her own seat, she begins crying out again.

"Let me help with the little one," a woman's voice says from behind me.

I struggle to find words to refuse when she sits beside me. "Thanks, but I don't think she'll let you hold her."

"Let me try." The woman reaches out and takes Molly in her arms, cradling her in her lap as I had. "Precious little angel."

It's dark. I can't make out this woman's face. Lights flash by the window, but they only make a kaleidoscope of her features. I start to turn on the overhead light.

"Don't worry so much, honey. I'll just sit here a while and let you have a rest. It'll be fine. You'll see." The woman beside me sings softly to Molly and rocks her gently.

I sit back, knowing I wasn't likely to fall asleep. "You must be somebody's mother."

"Five times over, honey. And a Nana, too. I got plenty of experience for sure. Heading home?"

"Yes, my mama's sick." I glance away before the tears come again.

"That's the place for you to be then, especially with this angel. She's bound to make anybody feel better."

"She hasn't ever seen Molly."

"Even more reason. Things bad between you?"

"Not anymore." I find myself telling this stranger about my life. It's dark, and it seems safe. I would probably never see her again after we leave the train. It's good to say it all out loud. I had never told another living soul about how things were.

"Poor child," the woman sympathizes when I've poured it out for her. "You've had a time of it. It'll be better now. Just you wait. Why don't you try to get some sleep, and I'll sit with this little one. Hush now. Don't worry."

I smile because I know I can't sleep. I have been through too much to fall asleep.

Besides I wouldn't leave Molly with a stranger, even if she was kindly and soft-spoken. Her voice is strange, oddly familiar, but I can't place it. I don't know her, and yet I feel completely at ease with her.

I turn my head to look out the window at the passing night that I'm running through to reach freedom. She sings to Molly again, and I close my eyes. I fall into a drowsy half-sleep. I'm aware that she is still beside me, aware that I am on the train, less than a hundred miles from home. I am warm and comfortable and feel loved like I haven't since I was a child. I knew that I was doing the right thing. I couldn't wait to put my arms around my family.

Despite everything, I fall asleep. I dream that I am at home in Mama's kitchen with the scrubbed table and the pot of beans always on the stove. Mama is making banana pudding. The smell of the bananas is so real.

When she looks at me, I smile at her. "I love you, Mama."

She presses her lips to my forehead and strokes my hair. "I love you, Ann. I will always love you, baby."

I wake up with tears trailing down my face. The train is slowing and the conductor calls out, "Charleston!"

The woman beside me carefully puts Molly back in her

seat. "I best be going now."

"Thank you," I say in a trembling voice. "I'd like to know your name."

But it's too late. She's gone. The lights come up in the car, and I look for her. She was a big woman, and I'm sure her hair was dark. But there's no sign of her.

I wake Molly, and we stumble out on the train platform. She waits quietly while I call my brother from a payphone.

"That woman who was holding me," she says when I was finished. "She told me she loved me and kissed my forehead."

"You must have dreamed it," I answer. "Uncle Zeke will be here soon. Then you'll finally get to meet Grandma."

Zeke pulls up in his old Chevy. I guess the woman with him must be his wife. I had so much to catch up on, so many secrets to learn. I introduce him to Molly.

He seems to be holding back. Of course, it has been ten years for him, too. I hug him tight, and he hugs me.

"Molly, this is your Aunt Fay. Mind taking a little walk with her for a minute while I talk to your Mama?"

Fay smiles at her, and Molly glances uneasily at me.

"It's okay, Molly." Fear is growing like a weed in my chest. Did Mama change her mind about me coming down to stay? Did Bobby already call and threaten them if they help me? I wait for him to speak with a sick feeling in my throat.

"It's about Mama," Zeke starts. "I didn't want to tell you on the phone. She died a few hours ago. She called out for you, Ann."

"She wanted to see you so bad before she went, you and Molly. She went quietly. She had this look on her face. She said she saw an angel. I just wish she could've seen you before she died."

I look around the train platform, but I know in my heart that I won't find that kindly woman who held Molly beside me on the train. I don't know why I didn't recognize her, even in the dark.

Something inside of me knew the truth.

Logic can hide the truth from us sometimes. Logic might never recognize that it was my Mama who sat next to me on the train that night. It was her only chance to hold Molly and say goodbye to me.

But I know the truth in my heart. I will never forget. I love you, Mama.

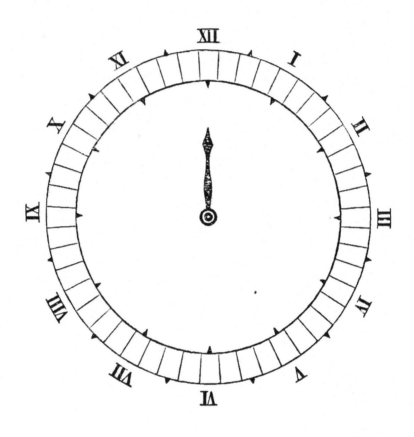

Spirit Warrior

What would you sacrifice for your community or your family? Jacks Jackson changes her whole life to find a killer among the natives in Those Who Walk in Darkness. In "Spirit Warrior," Tei is willing to give up even more for her people. We love a strong woman who follows her destiny, even if—make that especially if—it means going against what most people would expect of her.

When the other women had finally fallen into fitful sleep, Tei crept from the hut. The fierce wind took her breath away as she stepped into the night. In the darkness, the heavy snow glowed under the moon's dim light. The black trees swayed and whispered. She ran quickly towards the caves and their blue luminance just outside the village. She kept her head low in her heavy cloak, her reed shoes already frozen on her feet.

The caves were just inside the consecrated lands of the dead. No one ventured there. No trees grew. No plants; not even in the full heat of summer. Strange sounds, laughter, came from the empty lands but the Eganawe children were taught to ignore these things. They were the guardians of this place.

Tei shut her ears to the noise, kept her eyes on the path that led to the caves. Something pulled at her cloak and she ran, not daring to listen to the words that were whispered in her ears. She fell once in the snow, lost one of her shoes, but got up quickly. The snow froze on her face and hands where she had fallen. She bit her lip to keep from calling out as something shadowed and unreal loped alongside her, touching her hair, laughing at her tears of anger and pain.

She reached the cave, the warmth glowing from within to reach out and envelope her. Gratefully, she stepped inside, resting her face against the warm rock wall. It would mean her death to be caught there. No man or woman not chosen by the chiefs could enter these caves. Tei took a deep, steadying breath and started to crawl.

The rocky face of the walls and floor had been worn smooth with the passage of centuries. The warmth became stifling, hot air blasting out from the cave's interior. She kept her head low, her eyes on the growing light, hoping she would not crawl into the middle of them all with no chance to conceal herself. She could hear chanting as she went closer. An acrid smoke, nauseatingly sweet, filled the cave.

A sudden burst of blinding light preceded a long anguished cry of pain and horror that stopped Tei, leaving her trembling, just outside the huge cavernous opening. There were voices, whispered and hurried, then silence.

The mouth of the cave opened suddenly, yawning into a steep decline that dropped in well-worn ridges away from the sides of the wall. Light consumed the cavern. Grotesque shadows danced along the walls and the high ceiling. In the pit far below, a fire well spouted flames that had never died, sputtering blue and gold in the darkness. No one tended this fire. No wood or dried moss fueled its brilliance. Tei put up her hands to fend off its terrible heat, trying to find the others. She cringed against the wall on a ledge above them watching as they gathered around a fallen warrior.

"He is dead," one of the elder chiefs declared. "He could not be received into the spirit."

The other men drew back slightly. White Song, the young Eganawe chief, used his hand to smooth out the contortions on the twisted face. The pain had been intense, the death mercifully quick. "We must go on. At least one of us must be accepted by the spirit."

"Perhaps none of you is strong enough," the elder spat.

"I will be," White Song stated quietly but with a strength that vibrated through the cave. "I should have faced the test before him."

"We cannot lose you," the elder told him. "Better for Gray Willow to go next."

"Better for Gray Willow to take my place if I die," White Song answered. "I will be the next."

"As you will," the elder agreed after a moment, staring into White Song's sunrise eyes. "Make yourself ready."

Tei waited, eyes wide with fear, not breathing. It had been so long since any man had entered the caves to become spirit warriors that it was not even whispered among the women what this really meant. Perhaps the chief knew, she considered, watching intently as White Song disrobed and settled himself before the fire.

The elders began to chant. White Song closed his eyes and lowered his head, the blue gold fire glinted on his pale hair. His powerful muscles were tense, his hands clasped loosely at his sides. Tei put her hands to her ears as the chanting became deafening in the rocky cavern, echoing hollowly through her bones and vibrating in her brain.

A burst of white flame issued forth from the well. The flame engulfed White Song, dragging him to his feet, his arms thrown out towards the ceiling. His face glittered in the white light, his eyes open, gleaming with it. It roared around and through him. The elders fell to the floor, crying out in fear. Even the bravest warrior looked away from the terrible light that seemed to make White Song translucent near the fire.

Then it was gone, returning to the pit. White Song dropped to the floor, not moving. The others, slowly huddled around him.

Tei felt the tears on her cheeks, flooding her eyes. Was he dead as well? If White Song had not been accepted as a spirit warrior, what hope did the others have?

"Is he dead?" Gray Willow asked as the elders examined White Song's inert body.

"It appears so," they muttered together, shaking their graying heads.

"No!" Tei cried out, forgetting everything in her grief. Her words were drowned out by the return of the white fire, rushing out of the pit to inflame White Song's body once again. The others fell away in terror.

White Song got slowly to his feet. The fire retreated and Tei crouched low again in awe, grateful that they had not heard her cry. He was alive!

"You are well?" Grey Willow asked the chief.

"Better, my friend. My spirit is joined with that of the great warrior Mehmet. He is here with me, waiting to strengthen my arm and sharpen my eye."

The elders examined White Song, putting questions to Mehmet and nodding when they received their answers.

"Gray Willow," White Song put his hands on his friend's shoulders, "you must join me."

"Perhaps it is enough that only one of us is a spirit warrior," Gray Willow retorted, glancing around himself at the other warriors left in the cave.

"Perhaps he is right," the others agreed, not trusting the white flame that had nearly killed the chief and had killed one of their brothers.

White Song looked at his friends. "Come, you must simply be ready to accept and not show fear at the joining. It is not so big a thing."

"White Song," Gray Willow spoke for them all. "We cannot show courage in this. We can fight the Ngwa but we cannot do this thing."

"Besides," Morning Fire, one of the younger warriors exclaimed, "what is the proof that we would not all be risking our lives for nothing? You look the same, White Song. You speak the same. Perhaps you are the same. Perhaps the rest is illusion."

White Song strode to a huge boulder near the edge of the cavern. "Is this an illusion then, Morning Fire?" he asked as he lifted the rock far above his head. The group of younger men cowered back from him. He replaced the rock on the cave floor then hit it with his hand. The rock split cleanly in half.

Tei watched in disbelief. How could the others not be fighting to have such power? she wondered. If they would ask her...

"But you are right, my friend," White Song added. "It would kill you to be joined with a spirit if you are afraid. You must leave this cave and never return. Never speak of this to another. We will test the others. You must remain as you are."

It was difficult for Tei to tell if the men were relieved or ashamed. A few approached White Song as though they would change their minds. Gray Willow all but ran from that place. How would they live with their cowardice in the face of White Song's bravery? she wondered, carefully concealing herself before they neared the ledge where she hid. Who would fight beside him? Even though he was a spirit warrior and was capable of unbelievable feats, he could not fight alone. The Ngwa would overpower him with their numbers.

"I will let Gray Willow lead the warriors who do not find another spirit to attend them," White Song was saying to the elders as they came up from the pit. "Perhaps there is yet one more that can become Eganawe with the white flame."

Tei pressed close to the wall, listening as their footsteps echoed away from the cavern. She had seen the white flame and it had frightened her. But she had come there to become a spirit warrior, to fight beside White Song. Nothing had changed.

Slowly, she made her way down to the cavern floor.

From the perch high above, the well had looked much smaller. It was vast and higher than she was tall from the floor. She had never seen a stone like the one that formed its walls. There was a vibration against her hands as she touched it.

She did as she had seen White Song do and removed her garments, seating herself on the warm smooth rock floor. She emptied her mind of fear and thought only of fighting beside her chief. The flame roared in the well. Tei readied herself but the white flame didn't appear. She chanted as she had heard the elders do. There was no response. In anger, she scaled the high wall, standing on the edge of the stone.

"Come for me," she yelled into the pit. "I am ready. I want to be Eganawe. I want to be joined with a warrior spirit." There was still no response. The blue gold flame danced in the black hole.

The light burned Tei's angry eyes.

"What must I do?" she demanded. "Come for me. I have the courage to face you. You will not find me shaking with fear of you." The roar from the pit was deafening. The fire was cold and hot at once. Tei shook with helpless anger.

"If you will not come to me, spirits, then I will come to you."

Tei took a deep breath. There seemed to be no other way. Without further thought, she plunged into the well, her slender body disappearing into the fire.

The white flame soared up. From the mouth of the cave, White Song saw the illumination from the fire but did not stop to question its purpose.

Tei wasn't sure what happened to her. She screamed as the flames seared her body, expecting to hit something at the bottom of the well but there was nothing. The flames went on forever. Her mind seemed to float free of her body for a time. A thick haze held her suspended within the flame, falling. Yet there was nowhere to fall. Another world. Perhaps, she considered, this was death.

"Destroy her," a strange voice spoke clearly within her own mind.

"A girl," another added scornfully. "She cannot be joined."

"Perhaps," a third went on. "It has been done. I enjoin her spirit as I was joined. She is brave. Strong. She will fight for her people; for our people. I am Alleitha, spirit warrior. I will become one with her."

"You know the law," the first voice told them, Alleitha/Tei. "Your sacrifice is great."

The mists that shrouded her mind from her body lifted and Tei opened her eyes. She was no longer in the well of fire. She stood in the middle of a field, bronzed by the setting sun. Around her was the crying of the injured, the silence of the dead.

Gray Willow, his head nearly sliced from his body; Morning Fire, his quick, clever eyes forever closed. Blood was everywhere. From just behind her, she heard the cries of warriors still fighting.

She held out her hand and studied it. It was her hand but covered in a silver armor, holding a large silver blade. She heard the sound of White Song's war cry and ran on long, muscled legs that ate up the space.

Tei/Alleitha ran to where a large group of Ngwa were fighting an unseen opponent. White Song's war cry echoed from within that group.

"Cautiously, sister," Alleitha advised. "You are not prepared to do battle."

But Tei paid no heed using fist and blade to find her way to White Song's side.

White Song, bloodied and weary, looked up from the ground as two warriors were plucked aside like children. A silver blade shone in the sun.

"Rise, White Song!" Tei invoked. "You will not fight alone."

Mehmet, vanquished only as his host allowed, pushed

new strength through White Song's flagging body. "Alleitha! At long last. We stand together."

Together they fought on the rocky river's shore until their feet stood on the reiver's bodies and the brown river water ran red through the ice. One hundred times their number were defeated while a greater group ran to the east escaping into the shadows. Ngwa would long remember the terrifying giants who scourged their brothers. A few would plot revenge.

White Song looked at his companion as the Eganawe people cautiously began to spill from the village. Small fires glowed in the snow whitened landscape. The silver clad warrior was blood stained, shoulders bowed. "Brother," he laughed. "We have won for now. You saved all of us this day. Tell me your name. Show me your face."

White Song tried to peer beneath the dirty and shadowed helm but could only make out the eyes. Blue as the morning sky, courage and strength set deep within their surface.

"I must go," Tei began wearily to turn away. It had suddenly begun to occur to her what had happened, her head aching and body ready to fall despite her spirit warrior's strength.

White Song stared in disbelief. "We have fought together. We will eat together, smoke together. That is custom. Who are you?"

"I am not who you think I am, White Song," Tei replied, her voice sorrowful, her own yet strangely alien.

"We have become Eganawe, the only of our warriors to do so and survive. Ngwa will return. Do you leave me to fight them alone?"

Tei felt her heart melt at the sight of him, tall and golden in the firelight. "Let me help you, little sister," Alleitha offered and Tei accepted gratefully, unsure suddenly what to do.

"You will never fight alone," Tei promised, knowing that vow was etched in her soul. Her words hung in the air as she vanished into the night around them. The Eganawe people looked to the heavens. Surely they had witnessed a miracle. A warrior that was a gift from the sky sent to save them and their chief.

White Song sat beside a fire, brooding, not feeling wonder but great loneliness. So many had died. Many more were hurt too badly to survive the rest of the winter. He had released his warrior spirit when the battle had ended as Mehmet had shown him. They were joined only as White Song required. Perhaps, White Song considered, Mehmet would know the answer to the riddle. For now, he could feel a great weariness slide over him, pulling him down to the ground beside the fire. Later, he would consult the great chief.

Tei stood in the midst of her people, watching as they gathered wood to feed the fires that would burn until their enemies' bodies were consumed. Their own dead would be taken to the empty lands.

She was confused, frightened. What had happened to her? She remembered fighting beside White Song then afterwards as he greeted her she had heard her spirit warrior's offer of help.

"What's happened to me?" she asked aloud, looking at her arms and hands, not feeling the heat of the fires or the cold of the frozen night. The silver raiment she had worn was gone leaving her naked as she had been when she had jumped into the fire well.

"Alleitha," she called out. "Don't leave me this way." Several women carrying a dead Ngwa walked past her. Through her. Not seeing or touching. "How can this be?"

A woman, her hair long and black, her brown face smooth and beautiful came towards her. She wore no shoes and her garment was strange to Tei's gaze. "Hello, little sister."

"Alleitha?" Tei asked in wonder. "What has happened? Why can no one see or hear me?"

"Sit with me," Alleitha suggested. "Your path is hard before you, little sister."

"Please tell me," Tei urged.

"When you became one with me, little sister, you lost your physical form. You and I can become the warrior that fought at White Song's side today. Flesh and bone. But when we part, little sister, we become what we are now. Spirits in the realm of unreality. We can see and hear our people but we can never become part of their lives again."

"White Song..." Tei faltered.

"You saved his life today, little sister. Without you, he would be in the empty lands tonight. You must be content with that now."

"No," Tei argued angrily.

"You were not one of the chosen warriors that could be accepted...you could have been killed when you entered the white flame."

"Better that than to be punished for wanting to help my people," Tei answered. She raised her head slowly and looked as Alleitha. "This happened before...to you?"

"Long, long before, little sister," Alleitha smiled, sadness in her dark eyes. "I was as you rushing to fight when other warriors were too cowardly to face the white flame, to fight beside our chief Mehmet when he stood against another group of Ngwa in another bitter winter."

"And then you were parted?"

"Until this day when we fought again, I with you and Mehmet with your chief White Song. I have wandered in shame and sorrow until the time when you and I were joined. Mehmet is prevented by law from being with me in spirit form."

Tei ground her teeth. "This is foolish. We did nothing wrong besides being women in a time of need. We answered the call of our ancestors. This does not deserve punishment, Alleitha."

"How I wish there was another answer, little sister,"

Alleitha sighed.

"You and I can be joined, Alleitha." Tei jumped up from the ground. "We can stay as a spirit warrior, you with Mehmet and I with White Song."

"But White Song can never know that you are Tei." Alleitha warned, swift hope flooding her face.

"So be it," Tei agreed softly. "At least we will be together."

White Song sat in silence within his hut, considering the counsel that Mehmet had given him. The troubled young chief would rather have had a flesh and blood warrior at his side that day. The realm of the spirit was unknown to him and somehow frightening. He wanted his brother here beside the fire. There was so much to say, so many things had happened. The elders had been in awe of him and had never fought another living soul. They stayed a respectful distance and nodded approvingly. Angrily, White Song crushed a reed bowl in his hands then fed it to the fire.

"Peace, my brother," Tei greeted him from the shadow that surrounded the fringe of the fire light.

"You have returned," White Song narrowed his eyes to peer through the smoky light. "I thought that I would never see you again."

Tei/Alleitha sat down on the hard packed floor, Tei again astonished by the wiry muscle their combined bodies became in the joining. They were garbed in silver as before, a headpiece concealing Tei's features.

"Why did you leave, brother?" White Song demanded. "Are you flesh or spirit?"

"I am flesh, White Song," Tei replied. "But I am of the spirit."

White Song considered the cryptic words, wanting to appease his curiosity yet fearful that he would be alone again on this night if he did so. He nodded. "I will accept that. For now."

In the light of the dancing fire, they sat and talked of the battle that day. Several Eganawe entered the hut and just as quickly returned to the cold night. Their chief could speak with sky spirits but the rest felt unworthy.

"Some will return," White Song told Tei. "For vengeance. Some because they have no choice but to steal if they are to survive this winter."

"Perhaps we could meet the Vengeful ones with our strength and the desperate ones with our compassion," Tei said carefully. She could feel Alleitha's pleasure in her words.

"Perhaps." White Song managed a small smile. "You are wise as well as strong... will you tell me your name?"

The concealed face lowered briefly. "Know me by my arm beside yours, brother. I have no other name to give."

White Song's eyes of sunrise studied the still form on the other side of the fire. "I can sleep now, my friend. Will you be here when I awake?"

"I am here always at your side," Tei answered proudly. She lay down on the richly embroidered red quilt on the other side of the fire from White Song. The village slept around them.

Tei dreamed deeply, exhausted yet too full of everything that had happened to be still in her mind. Alleitha was there with her, her spirit comforting despite the pull she felt to leave her young charge. Would they be able to maintain their physical essence for all time? Alleitha did not know but she would try for Tei's sake as well as her own. She could see Mehmet in the young chief's fiery eyes.

Near dawn when the coldest winds whipped the trees and the tiny huts of the village seemed to cringe together, White Song had a dream. There was a young woman. He vaguely remembered seeing her in the village. She was wearing the garb that they had found in the caves near the fire well. Her long dark hair swept around her in the wind. He walked to where she stood, reaching out a hand to touch her pale face. He caressed her, smiling into her eyes. Eyes the color of the deepest summer morning.

Startled, White Song threw off his woven wrap, shivering in the cold, the fire nearly gone. He knew where he had seen those eyes before and the image haunted him. It wasn't possible. Yet he found himself stealthily climbing to where his companion slept, not sure what he meant to do, possessed by the dream and the feelings it had invoked.

Tei opened her eyes at his touch, not sure what was wrong until she realized that he had lifted the silver veil from her face.

The face White Song looked down on was the same as the one in the dream. "You are a village woman," he shook his head in disbelief. "How is this possible?"

Mehmet felt the pull of White Song's spirit and joined him looking into Alethea/Tei's face. "Alleitha, they have betrayed you," he whispered. For only an instant more in the dim light, the women were warrior joined. Tei/Alleitha reached out a slender hand. Then they were gone.

"What is happening?" White Song demanded. "Where did she go?"

Mehmet's spirit within him echoed his own remorse. He had seen his beloved Alleitha in the young woman just as White Song had seen Tei. "She is lost to me as she has been for longer that even I can remember."

"How could she have become a spirit warrior?" White Song wondered.

"She gave up her physical form just as Alleitha did to fight beside me. They were not warriors. They were not chosen. The spirits of the empty lands will not allow the joining now. They tricked you while you slept with a dream of her. Once it was revealed that she was a woman, Alleitha can no longer join with her to become solid flesh. They are trapped forever in the mists of the empty lands."

White Song raged even as the wind that ravaged the frozen land. "She they are to be punished for their bravery? We cannot allow this to continue, my brother."

"I know your thoughts, my brother," Mehmet's voice was like a sigh through White Song's mind. "But we cannot fight the elder spirits. The laws that bind our people to the empty lands and the guardians of the cave's knowledge are sacred."

"You may not fight them, my friend," White song threw on his woven cloak. "I fight for that woman who fought for me."

"What will you do, White Song?" Mehmet tried to counsel reason in the madness of his mind.

"There will be no more empty lands, no more caves of knowledge. No more spirit warriors," White Song answered, making his way to the caves.

"They will stop you, my brother. They are powerful."

"Then let them try."

Tei sat beside the fire well in the caves of knowledge, a gray shadow against the wall. She had been consumed by sorrow. Now there was only anger. The spirits of the well had told her that she and Alleitha would never join again. They would never become flesh. "Is this the knowledge of ages past?" she scorned. "Is this the wisdom we have guarded and died for?"

"Be thankful you have a life at all," the fire mocked her. "You could have been destroyed, body and soul."

"I am not thankful for your pitiful gift. Am I not as brave as any warrior? Am I not as willing to fight our enemies and defend your wisdom, oh mighty ones?"

"Little sister," Alleitha warned from the far side of the well.

"What can they do to me?" Tei demanded. "Let them take this half-life from me. You may be able to survive this way, my sister. I would as soon jump into the pit again."

The white flame roared up from the pit spitting at the ceiling, enraged and daring.

"You would not," Alleitha cried out, watching Tei as she jumped up to the top of the well again.

"They say we must not join again," Tei spoke to her quickly. "We must join if for one last time and end this for all. Come with me, Alleitha. They cannot harm us."

The flame raged wildly, calling with many voices. Warning, threatening. Alleitha moved quickly to Tei's side and with strength she didn't know that she possessed, she forced the forbidden union between herself and Tei.

Tei screamed in pain at the power that combined them, her disembodied voice echoing through the empty lands where White Song passed.

Mehmet, feeling the raw power that had been invoked as well as the angry call of the well spirits, urged White Song to the caves more swiftly. White Song, knowing Tei's voice intuitively, needed no urging. The flames raced through the caves creating blue fires everywhere. Shadows danced in the haze, taking on form and menace designed to keep Mehmet and White Song from the cavern.

"We will destroy this place," White Song promised, leaping back from the well as the angry spirits, already twice defied, retaliated, scorching his face and arms.

"They will destroy you as they have destroyed Alleitha," Mehmet told him.

"Let them come," White Song dared, not moving.

The white flame leaped from the well and overcame White Song, trapping Mehmet's spirit as well in the pain of their embrace. In the midst of the agony, White Song felt a touch, cool and protective on his brow. The flame changed, altering, shifting, until a barrier seemed to be formed around him. His eyes were burned by the fire. His throat and lungs were choked with it but he understood the nature of the change.

"Alleitha," Mehmet called, caught up in the void between the two women and the young chief trying to reach them.

Tei/Alleitha clung to their combined courage for one last time. They wrapped themselves tightly within each other's spirit. Then they leaped into the pit. The fury and agony of the flames burned them, uniting and destroying them as one. The white flame consumed them until they were one with it.

Mehmet howled within White Song's mind and the pain of loss transferred to him.

"We will destroy this place," White Song repeated, holding out his hands for the power of the white flame. "We will destroy you." The flame leapt obediently to his hand. Elder spirits fled before the power he wielded. He taunted them with the white flame that could destroy them as well, cruelly scorching their shadowed forms with the searing anger of the spirit fire controlled by Tei/Alleitha. The Spirits were trapped in the cave and the well of fire. Nothing of this kind had ever happened to them. They were repelled and impressed by it.

"What do you want of us?" their voices fractured against the stone walls.

"Release Alleitha and Tei. Allow them to join as warriors. Allow Tei to become a woman as I am a man when the joining is over."

"Free Alleitha's spirit," Mehmet added, ashamed of his own cowardice in the past yet proud of his young brother.

"Return the flame to the well," the voices pleaded. "We will do what you demand."

In the hollow of his hand, White Song felt the impression that was Tei absorbed by the flame. Would they honor their words? There was only one way to know. Putting his hand over the pit, White Song freed the flame. It burst upward, engulfing the cavern with warmth and light. The shadows disappeared and the white flame outlined a form not quite flesh and not wholly spirit.

Tei/Alleitha lifted her head as the fire returned to the pit. She stared unblinking into the sunrise eyes of White Song/Mehmet.

The young chief and the woman who loved him silently freed their spirit warriors then Tei laughed aloud as she felt his hand touch hers. She was whole and alive yet still Eganawe, ready to fight for her village and her chief. What was between her and White Song glowed in their eyes as they studied each other's faces without fear or embarrassment. And if in the many long nights that they would share, their warrior spirits joined them—Alleitha and Mehmet, warm flesh and soft sighs—Tei and White Song would smile.

About the Authors

Joyce and Jim Lavene write award-winning, best-selling mystery and urban fantasy fiction as themselves, J.J. Cook, and Ellie Grant. They have written and published more than 80 novels for Harlequin, Penguin, Amazon, and Simon and Schuster along with hundreds of non-fiction articles for national and regional publications. They live in rural North Carolina with their family, their rescue animals, Quincy - cat, Stan Lee – cat, and Rudi - dog.
Visit them at:
www.joyceandjimlavene.com
www.Facebook.com/JoyceandJimLavene

CPSIA information can be obtained
at www.ICGtesting.com
Printed in the USA
LVOW04s0927270316

480956LV00016B/427/P